by the same author

AGAINST THE STORM
THE FROZEN WATERFALL
WATCHING THE WATCHER

Coming Home

GAYE HİÇYILMAZ

faber and faber

First published in 1998
by Faber and Faber Limited
3 Queen Square London WC1N 3AU

Photoset by Avon Dataset Ltd, Bidford on Avon
Printed in England by Mackays of Chatham plc, Chatham, Kent

A CIP record for this book
is available from the British Library

ISBN 0-571-19367-6

2 4 6 8 10 9 7 5 3 1

For Timur, Kubilây, Hülâgü
and Mengü, with all my love

Contents

1 Under the Sun, 1
2 In the Shadow of Rocks, 14
3 A Change of Season, 25
4 A Moth at Night, 36
5 On the Swing, 47
6 At Home, 59
7 Family Life, 72
8 A Season of Gifts, 84
9 The Concrete Coast, 95
10 When Snow Falls, 107
11 Beneath the Surface of the Sea, 119
12 The Colour of Gold, 131

Glossary of Turkish words, 143

Under the Sun

It was extraordinarily hot on the beach. As the sun rose higher still, it was too hot to move and that was why Elif said that thing about never, ever, wanting to go back to England. She said it lazily, with her eyes shut against the intense glare and with the taste of salt and sweat on her cracked lips. Her younger brother, Atilla, who was sunbathing beside her, snorted and muttered, 'Dream on'. On her other side her brother-in-law, Refik Bey, who did not usually join them, cleared his throat.

'You don't have to go back,' Refik Bey said, putting aside his newspaper. 'You're old enough to leave school now, and you could, if you wanted to, if it was the right thing to do.'

'But . . .' Elif opened her eyes for a second. 'What would I do?' She could have glanced at her brother-in-law but the sun was too bright overhead and the air too heavy, and anyway, she wasn't keen to catch his eye. Even though Refik Bey was her elder sister's husband, and had been so for years, he still seemed like a stranger.

'You can stay with us,' he continued. 'You know you're welcome to, Elif. Very welcome indeed.'

Through hot, red eyelids she sensed him turn over and resettle his flesh on his towel. He would be exposing huge shoulders and the backs of his great, white legs to the midday sun. The rest of the family had withdrawn to the patch of shade under the balcony. Elif knew that she should have done the same.

Refik Bey had always been a well-built man, but in middle-age he was now more whale than man. In private Elif and Atilla told each other dreadful jokes about him, but afterwards Elif always felt guilty and took care that their sister, Sevim, never overheard. She knew that they shouldn't do it, but it was irresistible. They couldn't help themselves and sometimes nearly died of the laughter they struggled to repress. And he was such a generous man: really and truly generous. He was a distant cousin on her father's side but much more successful than anyone else in the family. He was seriously rich and had been inviting them all to this house by the sea, summer after summer, for as long as she could remember.

They had started coming years before Sevim had married him. In the beginning, Elif had always imagined that her sister had agreed to the marriage because of the house: Sevim must have calculated that marriage would extend this summer paradise for ever. But it hadn't been like that. The house by the sea hadn't been anything to do with it. Of all of them, Sevim was the one who liked the sea the least. She hated it, she said, now, and just couldn't bear the disgusting sand which got everywhere.

Poor Sevim. Sometimes she looked almost as old as Refik. That would be her now, putting the plates around the table, cutting up the loaves of bread with quick slashes of the knife and deftly scooping slices of golden aubergine from the boiling oil. She was so good at everything like that: a real Istanbul girl, everybody said, even if she had been born in the inland city of Ankara. Her origins hardly showed at all, Refik's mother insisted, now that Sevim had learnt to cook. Refik's mother, Zehra Hanım, liked food.

When it was hot in England, Elif always lost her appetite. Here in Turkey, it was different. She was constantly amazed

2

that even in this heat they could gather round the table several times a day, and eat and eat as though food was going out of fashion. Refik Bey said that sea air stimulated the appetite, while their own mother declared loyally that it was down to the skill of the cook. Sevim, returning to the table with yet another loaded plate, would flush in embarrassment and wipe the sweat from her forehead with the corner of her scarf. She never said much at all.

Since the birth of her two sons, Sevim had suffered from the heat dreadfully. She couldn't stand it. Recently doctors had said that she was allergic to the sun, and so should keep out of it altogether. Elif, in contrast, lived for it. She craved it and the attendant sea and beach. It was only the promise of it which seemed to keep her going in England. She dreamed of summer by night and then again by day. Back there in England, when rain leaked down for days on end and the skies were what she always thought of as 'English grey', she needed to remember this beach and the unfailing touch of the sun on her skin.

When she'd been little and in an English primary school, other children had always marked off Christmas on the calendar. They had decorated it with golden stars and crimson lines and rows of exclamation marks. Elif hadn't. She'd flipped through to the last week in July, and encased the last day of it in a brilliant, yellow sun. That was the day they returned to Turkey for their annual holiday; that was when she could pick up the threads of a life which was always torn off by their return to England at the end of each summer.

Now she gently touched the skin on her shoulders. She ought to have gone in. If she lay out here any longer she would burn, seriously. Then she'd peel and that would ruin everything. She'd made that mistake the summer before last. Her skin had flaked off so spectacularly that girls had crowded round in the changing rooms at school and begged to be allowed to peel a tiny bit off. And she'd let them, giggling with them at the fluttering, tearing sensation, even when it hurt. It had ruined her sun-tan so she really should seek the safety of the shade. At the very least she should go in and help Sevim with the lunch.

She could hear the older women hurrying between the kitchen and the table under the balcony, where they ate their meals. They were shouting to each other over the noise of sizzling fat dripping onto the charcoal grill. Suddenly they were arguing. One of Sevim's sons was protesting that something 'wasn't fair'; he wailed that he 'wasn't going'. She heard her own mother remark sharply that he was lazy, even if he was her grandson.

'I'm *not* lazy!' he shrilled. 'I just don't want to go!'

'All right,' Elif heard her sister say, '*all right*. I'll go.'

Refik must have heard her too because he stirred.

'Sevim?' he called, levering himself onto his elbows. He smelt strongly of coconut oil and something else as well.

'Sevim? Where are you going?'

'Nowhere,' she called down. 'Only to the grocer.'

'Why? What do you need from the grocer?'

'Bread, Refik. Your mother says that we need more bread. I'll be back in a minute. Then you can eat.'

'Why can't someone else go?' He was sitting up, busily cleaning the sand from between his toes. 'Are you sure we need more bread? If you'll just wait a minute, Sevim, I'll have a look for you. And you know you mustn't go out in the sun!'

He got up awkwardly and staggered back on the hot sand before stepping into green plastic beach shoes with surprisingly slim, white feet. Elif didn't look at Atilla but

4

continued to smile at the sun with her eyes tightly shut. Yesterday when Refik had clambered up the steeply shelving beach towards the house he'd sent an avalanche of dry sand and pebbles streaming down on top of them. Atilla had said something unrepeatable about water buffaloes. Refik Bey couldn't have heard him, but, just in case, Atilla had raced barefooted over the scorching sand to the sea. Then he'd dived in. When Refik had turned round to tell him to go and buy more bread Atilla had been twenty metres away and swimming strongly in the opposite direction.

Today was different. To Elif's astonishment, her brother jumped up and ran after his brother-in-law. Atilla, a stick of a boy with bleached hair that was too long, a friendship bracelet around his wrist, and three gold rings in his ear lobe, overtook Refik Bey.

'I'll go, Refik Abi. Let *me* go and get that bread for you.'

If Refik Bey was surprised he didn't show it. He extracted a fold of notes from the pocket of his shorts and counted the exact amount for three more loaves into Atilla's outstretched hand. He nodded agreeably as though he had always expected his wife's young brother to do the right thing, in the end.

Elif didn't move, but lay listening to Atilla's retreating steps. She would go in, naturally, but not yet. She would allow herself another moment under the unblinking regard of the sun.

Lunch would be ready. She could smell fresh peppers charring over the grill. Her sister would have split them open with her thumb and shaken the white seeds out before laying them in neat rows over the coals. Peppers were different in England: as heavy and green as garage paint and bitter as well. In the early years their parents had tried

5

to grow some in the back garden but it hadn't been a success. Now they didn't bother. Nowadays her mother was so busy in the shop that she didn't even bother to cook. Then they had take-away food: curries and Chinese stir-fries and fish and chips, followed by ice-cream. They ate ice-cream all the time, even in winter. Her parents still considered it a treat to have several enormous plastic boxes of the stuff filling up the freezer. It didn't taste of anything, but was soothing, in its way.

Then Elif shivered and opened her eyes in surprise. It was Refik. She must have dozed off. He had returned and was standing very close with his shadow all over her.

'I meant it, Elif,' he smiled down at her, stroking the edges of his beard. 'You'd be very welcome to stay with us. And you could be a great help . . . to Sevim.' He glanced back to where his wife was turning the meat on the grill. 'She does too much, don't you think?'

'Yes. I suppose she does. But I can't really stay, can I?' She wanted to get up and run indoors but couldn't with him standing so close. Instead she snatched up Atilla's towel and spread it over her legs. Her skin had begun to sting.

'I think I've overdone it,' she laughed lightly. 'I'm as burnt as those peppers!' Actually she felt chilled inside, as though the season had changed and no one else had noticed.

During lunch she felt so sick she had to leave the table to lie down in her room. Outside the older people were saying that it must be sunstroke and that a great big girl of sixteen, like her, should know better. They talked loudly, above the clatter of plates, and didn't care if she could hear. And it wasn't true. She wasn't sixteen yet, and wouldn't be until a month after they returned to England.

That return journey was only two days away and the

6

thought of it made her more miserable. It was the same every year. Before they came she and Atilla decided to do something special each day. They wouldn't waste time. They'd go into town regularly and visit the castle and the museum. They'd go on boat trips to the islands with other, proper, tourists. They could even join a tour to Pamukkale. It wasn't far away. Lots of people from school had been, whereas Elif, who had been born in Turkey, had only seen its pictures on postcards. And this year they would definitely take a picnic up to the ruined amphitheatre on the slopes of the hill above the house. Lying side by side amongst old, smoothed stones, they'd breathe the scent of crushed thyme and the few remaining orange groves. Below them the sea would stretch beyond the headland and as they dozed in the bleached, dry grass they would watch the flickering horizon. But they didn't do it. Those days of endless sun had flashed by like shoals of glittering fish and now it was too late.

Suddenly there was barely time to plan the shopping trip for souvenirs. Elif decided not to bother. She and Atilla began to stay on the beach later and later each day and sometimes, when everyone else had gone in for the evening, they swam out through reddening waters towards the setting sun. They moved slowly, languidly even. The sun was so low and bright that it blinded them and they could barely think of anything at all.

During those final days, Elif usually agonized about what to take back as presents for girls in her class. It was expected of her, but had been getting more difficult each year. She used to buy rings and necklaces made from the blue glass beads which keep off the 'evil eye'. Friends had liked these, at first. Then she had bought little camels and donkeys made from brass, then dried gourds painted to look like real people. Now her friends wanted more sophisticated gifts. She had glanced around the town but this year came home empty-handed. Everything had been so expensive. She was convinced that people asked a higher price, because they recognized her as a summer visitor with too much foreign money who could afford to be cheated.

Now she wouldn't trouble, or would only buy bottles of cologne at the airport. Then, at least, no one could complain of being left out. And if she didn't feel better tomorrow, she wasn't going to even bother with that.

She must have dozed off, then was wide awake. The room was dark. She was aware of the clammy sheet covering her and sweat on the back of her neck. She wasn't alone. A figure stood by the window. How long had she slept? Was it tomorrow already?

'Mum?'

Somebody was clumsily drawing the curtains, darkening the room still further.

'It's only me, Elif. I only wanted you to sleep – .' It was Sevim. Now Elif made out her sister's face, pale and unmoving beneath the white scarf which tied away her hair. 'Go back to sleep. I just – '

'Just what?'

'Nothing. Nothing at all. How are you feeling? That was all I wanted to know.' Sevim didn't come over to the bed. They weren't that close. 'I'll leave you to sleep. It's the best thing, sleep. Only Refik did say, well, mentioned really, that you were thinking about staying on . . . with us. He said that you wanted to help, to help me, that is, with the baby. Of course, I said that you couldn't possibly. But you know what men are like, once they get an idea in their heads. So I'll let you sleep.' She didn't move, just retied the scarf more securely. 'It's just that Refik worries about me – that I

8

do too much!' She gave a faint little laugh. Elif switched on the light. 'Of course I understand that you couldn't even if you wanted to, because Mum and Dad wouldn't let you! Though Mum did say that they wouldn't mind if you didn't finish your education. It's not everything, is it? I mean, look at me. I didn't finish my education. But I know you wouldn't want to give it up . . . not for . . . me.'

Elif didn't know what to say. She wanted to ask 'what baby?' but she suddenly saw it, outlined there as her sister stretched up to jerk nervously at the edge of the curtain. She saw the bulge on her sister's body, where yet another child was growing. Sevim ran her hands anxiously over her plain, white face.

Then something smashed on the concrete outside. Refik's mother, old Zehra Hanım, shrieked and called for help, for someone to come and save her! At once.

'It's only *cats*, Granny.' That was Atilla's voice.

'And it's your own fault, Mother,' Refik added, tolerantly. They must have all been sitting out there, watching the sea in the dusk. 'You encourage the brutes by putting out scraps. No real harm's been done. Better a couple of broken glasses than a broken limb! But that mess will have to be cleared up.'

'I'll do it,' offered Atilla, uncharacteristically.

Zehra Hanım was ordering him about, warning of the terrible consequences of a cut: even the smallest scratch could lead to blood poisoning and before you knew it, you had gangrene and a foot had to be cut off, or a leg or two, if you'd been really careless. The sisters listened to the crunch of glass and the rasp of the brush on the dry concrete. Zehra Hanım continued to complain that she could feel fragments of glass on the soles of her slippers. Refik Bey sighed, then he complained about the newspaper article he was reading.

9

'Those muck-raking journalists should be hunted down like vermin,' he grumbled. Eventually peace was restored but beyond, the wild cats yowled and fought in the night.

'How do you put up with them?' asked Elif. She had heard Atilla's sharply indrawn breaths as he struggled to control his temper, and was amazed that he was not already cursing in English.

'It's not a problem,' said Sevim, twisting and untwisting the corners of her scarf. 'Anyway, they're family, so what can I do?'

'You're an angel,' said Elif. 'That's what Mum and Dad should have called you: Angel. If Zehra Hanım was my mother-in-law, I'd push her down the well!'

'We don't have a well. And maybe you're running a temperature. Do you think Refik should get the doctor?'

'No, I'm fine. And I didn't mean that, about the well . . .'

'Didn't you?' asked Sevim.

She left abruptly on silent, stockinged feet and when the door had closed behind her the room refilled with the sounds of other people's lives. An outboard motor throbbed across the bay towards the headland and along the coast road cars braked and hooted as they approached the bend below the castle. Now and again the cats still screamed. Briefly, as the night breeze ebbed and flowed, she heard dance music from the clubs that had sprung up to serve the summer visitors. The conversations from outside grew quieter and her two nephews, Hakan and Volkan, allowed themselves to be led away to bed without too much protest. Around the light a mosquito began its high-pitched drone.

Elif looked at her watch. It was still the same day. Tomorrow would still be the last but one day, and the day after that the last of all, and not a proper day at all. It would be a spread of hectic hours laid out like stepping stones, which she must balance on as she prepared to return.

It would be raining in England, and cold, even though it was only September. Her friends might not like lemon cologne: she imagined them opening the bottles and dabbing it on their wrists. They'd wrinkle their noses, frowning at each other out of the corners of their eyes. 'What is this foreign muck?' That's what they'd think, even if they didn't say it. It had happened when she'd brought back boxes of Turkish delight. It had been 'the real thing', dark coloured, with nuts embedded in its uneven, hand-cut squares. It wasn't even sweet. Her friends, who were used to something pink and scented which had always reminded Elif of bathroom soap, had been horrified. Her best friend, Claire, pretending she'd bitten her tongue, had spat hers out onto the playground. So maybe the cologne was another bad idea.

Later that night one of her nephews stirred and called. Someone got up. It would be Sevim again, padding across cool stone floors on bare feet. She would be bending over her little son, with this other baby growing within her. Her own sister, who was not yet twenty-five, was expecting a third child! It made Elif feel odd.

Their mother, Filiz Hanım, was proud of being the 'young' grandmother of two fine grandsons. She rather looked down on English women of her age who were only just beginning their families. Did she know about this coming baby? And did Zehra Hanım? It was difficult to believe that the old woman could have kept such a secret: if anyone had hiccups, she liked to know.

Had Refik and Sevim confided in her, alone? Upstairs a door closed. Poor old Sevim. Was she pleased? No wonder Refik had asked her to stay. But she couldn't: it was impossible. She wasn't sure that she wanted to. Not seriously.

She imagined their house back in England. It always looked unbelievably small and poky when they returned. Her father would unlock the front door and they'd step in over a huge, accumulated pile of letters and adverts. Once inside they'd smell the warm, shut-in air. They'd see the dust and the dried up flies on the window ledges. Elif always felt cold. She'd shiver and run upstairs for a jumper to pull on over her sunburnt arms. Once in her room she would be surrounded by all the things that belonged to England: posters mended with sellotape and the cuddly animals which girls give to each other as presents. She would switch on her computer which her parents were so proud of and which had cost them so much money. She would phone friends to hear all the latest gossip.

She was disturbed again: the bolts were being drawn back on the side door. The key turned stiffly in the old lock. Could Zehra Hanım be getting up for the first prayers? But it was too early and still pitch black outside. Anyway, those were young footsteps, and they were hurrying towards the beach. Elif went to the window.

'Sevim?' There was no reply. Had something been forgotten on the beach? What was so important that poor Sevim must go and search for it in the middle of the night?

'Sevim, is that you?'

No steps returned. The sea would be waiting there unseen on the dark edge of the sand, for there was no moon tonight. Maybe her sister just wanted to be out of the house in the cool of the night, when the sun was safely away and no one could ask anything of her.

'Sevim?' Elif had tried to call quietly, without disturbing the whole house, but now, she was alarmed. She ran towards the sea calling her sister's name again and again. She crossed the sand where they had lain that morning and it was now cold. Splashing through the shallows she kicked something that hurt so much she stumbled and fell. When she had struggled to her feet she heard the steady stroke of someone swimming close by.

In the Shadow of Rocks

Elif stood absolutely still. It wouldn't be one of her family, but a stranger, someone quite unknown, who was swimming across the bay before dawn. People did the oddest things in the holiday season, especially the tourists. If she didn't move they might not notice her. When they had swum past she would slip back indoors. There was no one on the beach. She had been mistaken. She must have dreamt of doors unbolted and feet hurrying to escape into the night. Perhaps Sevim had been right and some fever was disturbing her sleep. She certainly felt very hot and the water was as deliciously cool as silk slipped around bare limbs.

She let her feet sink into the soft, wet sand. The unseen movement of the waves touched the hem of her night-shirt, dragging it to and fro. Then, in the east, the red sun began to rise up beyond the headland. A single call to prayer trembled, strengthened and finally swung round the bay. In the hotels sleeping holiday-makers would stir restlessly at the unaccustomed sound. In little houses on the hillside people would already be up and the work of the day would soon begin. In the water the swimmer drew nearer. As Elif stood there, screwing up her eyes and trying to see, night was slowly torn back. Under the headland the shadows of daylight began to creep from the base of the rocks.

Atilla didn't see her until the last moment. He was already in warmer, shallower water and his feet had brushed against one of the sandbanks. He had swum more than half-way to the island, then promised himself to return in fewer than three hundred and fifty strokes. As the light flowed back he strung the strokes out luxuriously, gliding through the water and almost letting himself sink too deep before sweeping himself forward again, into waters dyed red and gold.

When he angled his head to draw in another lungful of air he sensed something in front of him. Something was too still amongst the slippery movement of the sea at dawn. He faltered. The sudden chill of a new current of water enclosed him and bound his chest like tightening bands of wire. He felt it in his heart and was unable to breathe, unable to free himself. For a second he thought his enemies had caught him. They had threatened that they would. When he'd told them that he didn't care about their threats because he was spending the summer miles away, where they could never find him, they'd laughed. They'd spat in his face and messed up his hair. Then, hustling him up against a wall on the far side of the playground, Price had asked, 'What's a summer?' Price, who had spots, had squeezed something on the back of his neck. 'What's a summer', he had repeated, 'when winter's to follow? It'll be dark by five, very dark indeed! So what does Atilla the Ant think about that?'

'Anyway,' Hooper had joined in, 'who says Turkey's miles away? My dad has a mate with a yacht in Turkey. In some posh marina, it is. He's given us an invite and my dad's keen. And so am I . . . I've heard that Turkish girls are *really* hot. So don't get me wrong, mate. It's not *all* Turks I hate. It's just you, Atilla: you're so sad and you make me so mad. I don't know what to do about it.' He had sniggered and the others, who stood around, joined in. Then Price had glanced at his finger and thumb and flicked something at him before wiping the rest on his shirt-tail. Hooper had lunged. He'd put his head down and gone for Atilla who had flinched and avoided most of the blow. Then he'd run. They had jeered. They'd stamped their feet and pretended to give chase but they hadn't bothered to go far. They'd crashed into one another, panting for breath, choking with laughter and screaming abuse but that was all. Atilla had run and run until the noise of the afternoon traffic and his own bursting heart were all that he could hear.

Later he had found his way back home. The next day he hadn't gone in to school but had killed time in the park, and nobody had noticed.

Now his fractured stroke dragged him so deep that the whole weight of the cold ocean was crushing him to death. He feared he was drowning and thrashed out in panic but couldn't call with his throat full of water.

'Atilla!' Somehow she caught hold of him and clung on, falling backwards under the burden when she felt the pebbles beneath her feet. She tipped him over onto his side and when he began to cough and retch she let him go. He crawled in front of her on his hands and knees. There were bubbles of foam on his lips and nose. Then he threw up like a dog.

Up at the house somebody was folding the shutters back, letting in the pink dawn. A cockerel from the village houses on the other side of the main road began to crow. Elif squatted on the sand beside her brother. He was shaking uncontrollably.

'What happened?' she asked. 'Did you get cramp again?'

'Yes.'

'Then why did you swim alone? Especially at night. You are so stupid, Atilla.'

16

He wouldn't look at her. His teeth were chattering and his skin was mottled with purple.

'I was only going half-way to the island,' he stammered. 'We've done it loads of times.'

'You're not just stupid, Ati, you're – ' She couldn't quite think what he was.

He shrugged and rubbed his hands over his blue lips.

'But you were alone, weren't you?' She needed to prove his stupidity to him.

'Alone?' He glanced quickly around. 'Of course I was alone. Who's stupid now?'

He sat up and squeezed water from the ends of his long hair. Scowling at her, as sulky and beautiful as any seven-year-old, only he wasn't seven now. He was thirteen, but still beautiful, and he always had been. He was the most beautiful thing Elif had ever seen. She'd loved him instantly. She could still remember her first glimpse of him. She had expected to dislike this baby because everybody had said that she would be jealous, but she hadn't been. She'd loved him. And she'd almost brought him up. People said that she was more of a mother than a sister to him, even though she was barely three years older. It was a good thing that she'd taken to him because their mother had been too busy for this third child and Atilla had needed a great deal of bringing up, especially in school in England.

As the sun rose higher the morning haze evaporated and they could see the outline of the island. It had never had a name. Local people called it 'Taşlı Ada', which meant 'rocky island', but recently the council had renamed it 'Altın Ada', or 'Gold Island'. Ahmet Efendi, the gardener, didn't approve. He said that there wasn't the slightest trace of gold out there and the name only sounded exciting to strangers. Certainly, there were regular boat-trips to it and people said that tourists were sunbathing nude on the far side. On a clear day you could just about see people diving from the overhang at the south end. That was the only safe place. Elsewhere the turquoise waters rippled over sharp, black rocks that were nearer to the surface than people thought.

The island wasn't that far away. Elif had swum over several times in previous years, though never alone. They had always made a party of mainly women and children and swum in a leisurely fashion, resting from time to time in Ahmet Efendi's boat. He acted as caretaker, gardener and handyman and looked after the summer house for Refik Bey. He rowed steadily and powerfully and when she was little his calloused hands with their deeply split flesh and broken nails had reminded Elif of the crabs that hid amongst the rocks. She had been a little scared of him. Ahmet Efendi's faded eyes were lost beneath wrinkles so deep, that she could never tell where he was looking, but he'd always brought them back unharmed.

This year they hadn't done the trip to the island. Refik Bey was against it. Things had changed, he said. It wasn't only that Ahmet Efendi and his boat were both too old, it was the tourists, too. Elif had protested, but Refik Bey had insisted: the rocks were covered with all sorts of filth and he didn't want his family seeing things like that.

Elif and Atilla had been disappointed. The trip had been part of the cargo of memories which she carried back to England. She used to pack those summer experiences away with the beach towels and flip-flops and half-used bottles of sun oil. Occasionally, on the endlessly wet evenings of winter and spring, she would examine them secretly, and finger the sand that lay in the corners of things.

'It's still stupid,' she said. 'If you wanted to go so much, why didn't you ask me? Then you wouldn't have been alone.'

'It doesn't matter,' he scowled. 'Don't fuss. You wouldn't even have known if you hadn't got in my way like that. I'd have been all right, if it hadn't been for you! You nearly drowned me!'

'I didn't! Anyway, you said you had cramp, and that wasn't anything to do with me! You should be glad I was here. Next time I hope you drown!'

'I didn't get cramp.' His voice had changed.

'You could have fooled me! So you're a liar as well as stupid!' She heard herself sounding exactly like some teachers at school but he didn't seem to have noticed.

'Elif Abla,' he whined. He was hunched up, hugging his knees. His backbone stuck out from his smooth skin like a row of loosely sewn on buttons. She longed to put an arm around him but didn't. They were too old for that.

Up at the house someone had come out into the garden. They heard the water splash from the hose onto leaf and stone, then run down the steps. It would be Ahmet Efendi or one of his grandsons. Most of his children were working in Germany, but they still sent their children back to the village from summer to summer. The smell of water on dusty stone and dried earth floated down to Elif. Sometimes, though very rarely, she had noticed it in England, when sudden rain pattered down into an afternoon that had promised to be long and fine. It was almost her favourite smell and reminded her instantly of summer in Turkey.

'Look at that!' Atilla leapt to his feet, pointing.

'What?' She couldn't see anything. He crouched behind her, gripping her shoulder, forcing her to look.

'There!' he cried. 'There!'

A yacht was rounding the overhang on Taşlı Ada. Its sheets flapped as it failed to change tack. It was too close.

'Tourists,' said Elif and yawned. There were often accidents out there.

'No!' protested Atilla but it almost certainly was. Local people knew about the rocks; only strangers went so close. He was shading his eyes intently.

The boat hung and shuddered as though already caught, then some breeze that blew out there but not on the beach gathered slowly in the white sail. It filled, then tightened and the yacht slid into the deeper channel that would take it safely to the harbour. As Elif watched it glide past, curls of music spun from it over the water and when somebody on deck waved, she waved back. Atilla cursed, and pushing her roughly aside ran back into the house.

Finally, unavoidably, it was the day before the last day. At breakfast the atmosphere had already changed. No one lingered. Her mother barely finished two glasses of tea before announcing that this year she was going to get all the packing done early. Elif knew it wouldn't happen. Filiz Hanım always wasted the day fussing about things that didn't matter at all and then stayed up all night. It was the same every year. It was as though they all pretended that they weren't leaving.

Only Hatice Teyze, Ahmet Efendi's wife, seemed unperturbed that the house would soon be emptied. She sat comfortably on a low wall and peeled hard boiled eggs into an enamel basin.

'You won't find anything as fresh as this in England,' she remarked. She often visited her children in Germany but preferred life in Turkey. Now she dipped the end of an egg into the salt and held it out to Atilla between fingers stained brown with henna. He shook his head.

'Here,' she tried again. Elif relented and took the egg, though she didn't really want it. She knew that Hatice Teyze would do anything for her; she would have even spread butter and honey onto slices of bread and fed them to her as though she were a tiny child still. Hatice Teyze considered Elif to be dangerously thin. No man, she said, would want a wife so thin. Each summer she tried to fatten her up.

In front of them the turquoise sea glittered in the sun. As the temperature rose, the outline of the island shimmered and in the distance the horizon slowly dissolved.

'Do you remember the name of that yacht?' Atilla asked suddenly. He was arranging olive stones in a pattern on his plate.

'No. I don't think I saw it. But I heard their music. Would you like to go into town and look for it in the harbour?' It seemed like a good idea but he stared at Elif in horror.

'No!' he shouted. 'I would *not!*'

'OK. It was only an idea, Ati . . . Well, *I* might go. They looked really friendly. And they waved.'

'They *waved*?'

'Yes. And I waved back.'

'You didn't – '

'I did. Why shouldn't I?'

Then she saw that his hands were shaking so much that he'd knocked the pattern out of shape.

'What is it, Ati?'

He wouldn't look at her, but hunched himself up and sniffed.

The others left to pack and there was only Hatice Teyze stacking the dishes onto a large brass tray. She knocked the wasps away and tossed the scraps over the wall for the cats.

'I can't go back,' he muttered.

'What do you mean?'

'I *can't* go back to England. Ever!' His voice was shrill with tears only just held in. 'I can't, Elif. They'll get me, if I do. They said they would, as soon as the evenings are dark.'

'What are you talking about?' She didn't understand at all.

'It's Price mainly, Stuart Price and his friend Hooper and some others at school. They *hate* me! They're out to get me. Honestly, Elif.' He was whining again. 'They'll hurt me, Elif.'

'How long's this been going on?'

'Ages. Well, it's *always* happening. You know: people calling me "a filthy Turk" and stuff like that, but it's been really bad since . . . since . . .'

'Since?'

'How do I know? Since . . . half-term.'

'Why didn't you tell the teachers?'

'I did.'

'And?'

'And nothing. They don't do anything, do they?' He avoided her eyes.

'Then you should have told me, Atilla. I'd have helped you.'

One year she had had trouble. A group of girls had followed her around saying 'gobble, gobble, gobble', but she'd complained at once. A teacher had talked to them and it had stopped. One of the girls, Claire, had become a best friend. Claire had only wanted to have fun.

'I'll come with you when we get back. You've got to say something.'

'I already have – but you don't believe me. Honestly, Elif, you're as bad as them. You think I'm making it up too.'

'I don't!'

'You do. I can see it on your face.'

'You can't!' She knew he was being unfair.

'If you believed me, you'd help.'

'I *will* help.'

'You won't.'

'I will. I'll do whatever you want.'

'Then say you won't go back, Elif. Please! If you stay, they'll let me stay, too.'

Her heart missed a beat.

'I can't do that, Ati.'

'There!' he screamed. 'I *knew* you wouldn't help. But I still won't go back, Elif. I'll run away, or kill myself. And it'll be your fault.'

'Mum and Dad wouldn't let us stay.'

'They will: and it's only for a year, isn't it? Or two. Aren't they always saying, "Just another year in England, then we'll have enough money to return".'

'But . . .'

'And Refik Abi wants you to stay. He said so, on the beach.'

'But he doesn't want you! You can't stand each other.'

'I can. I've changed. Look how nice I was yesterday.'

'That's different. That was yesterday. This is forever. And . . .'

It was as if some door was being opened very, very slowly and through the widening gap she was seeing some vista that she had only dreamt of before.

Hatice Teyze reached between them and stroked Elif's cheek affectionately before collecting the last two tea glasses. She always wore the same patterned dress over faded blue şalvar. She must have washed the clothes at night and taken them from the line again each morning.

They'd brought her loads of things from England, but she never wore them, always saying that she was keeping them for best. She'd patched this dress several times, and by hand. Now she paused, with the tray balanced on her hip, and drew a finger over Atilla's upper lip.

'Next year,' she said, 'I want to see a moustache.'

'I'll try,' he said in Turkish and blushed. Hatice Teyze laughed, patting him on the shoulder and calling him 'aslan' – 'lion'. For a moment he forgot and laughed like the dear little boy he had once been.

Elif went upstairs. Her parents weren't actually packing but were standing on either side of the bed which was piled high with things they wanted to take back.

'Mum,' she began, 'it's Refik Abi. He's asked me to stay . . . sort of . . .'

They remained silent, but exchanged a careful look. Her mother folded up another towel.

'I can't possibly, can I . . . ?' faltered Elif.

Then she heard her father begin to speak.

'Well, dear, if that's what you *really* want, I don't see why you shouldn't stay. Do you, Mother? After all, she's a big girl now!'

3

A Change of Season

As that day drew to its close it seemed to Elif that her parents spent more time deciding what to put in the empty spaces in the van than in considering their children's future. The decision to stay had happened with no discussion at all. Now, too swiftly, there was a leave-taking like no other.

Even while she helped her mother and father load up, Elif couldn't believe that she wasn't going with them. It had been too sudden. Her parents had acted as though bewitched. They had agreed to something that had been no more than a moment's idle thought on a hot beach at midday. Elif wondered if her brother-in-law had already spoken to them about her. They firmly denied it.

'No, dear,' her mother had said, 'as though he'd suggest such a thing! You know how important he always says education is. But if it's what *you* really want, Elif, then your father and I won't stand in your way.'

Her father smiled his agreement.

'And Atilla?' Elif asked hesitantly.

'Now that's another matter.' Her mother had stopped what she was doing. She folded her arms across her chest and made a fuss about Atilla: she wasn't so sure they could spare him.

Elif lied for him. She remembered his terror when he spoke of his unhappiness in England and she found herself saying, 'But the thing is, Mother, I think *I* might need him.

You know what people are like here, about a girl on her own . . .'

'Exactly!' cried Refik Bey, rubbing his fingertips lightly over his beard. 'I didn't want to mention it, but since you've brought it up, Elif, I have to say I think you're absolutely right. This isn't England and a young girl can't be too careful! You'll need your brother. And I dare say we can fit him in.'

Only her father had wavered. On the last evening he still threatened to come back and get his son if he 'stepped out of line'. In England father and son had not always got on.

'I won't be any trouble. I promise, honestly!' Atilla had been very persuasive and in his new role as Elif's responsible brother he had gone straight down to a barber's and had his long bleached hair shaved off. After that, there wasn't much room for argument. Atilla had spent the entire holiday disregarding demands that he 'get a decent man's haircut'. Now they were all impressed.

The only discordant notes were struck by Hatice Teyze and Ahmet Efendi. He always helped to load up, carrying the heavy tins of white cheese and tomato paste out to the van and bringing them melons from his own garden. Each year they took these back to England and they lasted well into the winter. The old man had always secured the luggage on the roof-rack, skilfully tossing the ropes to and fro over the irregular load of cases and cans of water and last minute gifts from relatives and neighbours. He was a tough, agile worker, who could turn his hand to anything. Now, on the morning of their departure, he wasn't around. He had left before the sun was up, returning to his village in the mountains, where there were 'unexpected family problems.' No one believed the story. Hatice Teyze remained impervious in the kitchen, quickly rolling out the rounds of dough for the home-made pide, which she considered vital food for any journey.

'People are asking me for jobs all day long,' Refik Bey complained at the kitchen door. 'If Ahmet Efendi can't do a full week's work, there are plenty who can. Suppose I needed the car cleaned, or that van?' He looked over at the vehicle and its load. The old woman sent the long, thin rolling pin rippling across the dough. She scooped a handful of flour from the sack and scattered it over generously. Refik Bey stepped back. Later they'd seen her running her own duster over Refik Bey's car. Her little grandson, Noyan, had squatted near, polishing the gleaming hub-caps.

Elif had also been upset by Ahmet Efendi's absence. When she'd told him she was staying on, he had looked up in disbelief. Then he'd resumed work more vigorously only muttering something about Istanbul being a dangerous city.

'But now we can do the trip to the island, can't we, Ahmet Efendi?' She had smiled at him persuasively. 'We can do it after they've gone, and I know you've always enjoyed it. We could take your grandson, couldn't we? And Hatice Teyze . . .' She had kept on talking to hide her disappointment at his disapproval.

'We could have another barbecue: catch fish on the way over and grill them on the rocks. It was so lovely when we did that. We could do it again, couldn't we? Before I go to Istanbul?'

'We could,' he said, but so reluctantly that she knew it was never going to happen. He was weeding flower beds at the front of the house. He kept moving along so that she had to move too. There really weren't any weeds, so he needn't have worked so hard. He could have stopped and talked to her properly like he used to. His grandson, who was playing close by with a tin can, regarded Elif impassively. He was a silent child, who didn't speak much Turkish because he had only recently arrived from Munich.

'Aren't you pleased I'm staying?' she asked in desperation. It was a silly question, but his resistance hurt. She had expected him to smile and say, 'Maşallah: God Bless you! What good news!' Instead he had looked perplexed. Until that moment she had always thought that she and Atilla were special. Now Ahmet Efendi didn't appear to approve of her at all.

She couldn't believe that the van was about to drive away for another whole year, and that he wasn't even here to open and close the gates for them. As Elif and Atilla stood side by side, Refik Bey laid a moist hand on both their shoulders. Sevim stood apart in the shadow of the house, watching; her two sons squabbled over something one of them had found. Old Zehra Hanım muttered prayers and beckoned for Hatice Teyze to throw down a basin of water so that the journey to England might be as smooth as that easy flow. Her father started the engine, accelerated, then stopped and leant from his window.

'That's my insurance that you've got there, Refik!' He smiled at his son-in-law. 'So look after them properly. They're the only insurance that we'll ever come back!' He laughed cheerfully, so that everyone would know that it was a joke. Her mother looked back, pushed away a tear and waved to them both.

'Look after yourselves, and don't be a nuisance,' she called. When the van moved on again she rested her head back and stretched out her legs. The van turned out of the gates. Sevim was frowning anxiously against the bright light.

They listened to the horn as her father sounded it all along the coast road. Finally, beneath the castle, the van rounded the bend.

'Thanks,' said Atilla, before they went in. 'Thank you *so* much!'

'That's all right,' said Refik Bey comfortably, 'Just go and shut the gates, there's a good lad. Properly.'

As Atilla hurried off, Elif realized that her brother hadn't been thanking her at all.

Two days later Refik Bey took his family back to Istanbul. They weren't going direct but were stopping on the way at the factory in Bursa. He had to see how things were going there. They were in the middle of a big clothing contract with the Middle East. That was why he couldn't take Elif and Atilla with them. But he'd be coming back for them, as soon as he could.

For the first few days Elif couldn't believe that she hadn't returned. She kept imagining school and her empty place at the table. Her friends would ask questions about where she was. On Saturdays they'd go to the discos without her. They'd even ask another girl instead, so that they could share the taxi home at night. But Emma and Claire would be absolutely devastated by her absence, and jealous. There was no doubt about that. Claire, especially, had been trying to leave school for ages, but her parents would not hear of it, not in the middle of GCSEs. She began a letter to Claire, trying to explain what had happened, but she couldn't finish it; she wasn't quite sure why she had stayed and now that Sevim had gone, she sometimes felt uneasy.

Lying on the beach she imagined her parents on the long journey northwards to Istanbul, then on across Europe to the English Channel. It had always been an endurance test. Elif usually slept. She was amazed that she could sleep for hours on end, but there never seemed much else to do. She'd given up looking at the sights long ago. Atilla, slumped in his corner, always listened to tapes, jiggling his

29

shoulders or jerking his head from side to side. Elif just sat. There wasn't much to talk about either: after all, they'd just spent an entire month in each other's company so there was no news or gossip. It was only a matter of getting home in one piece. The routes which the returning migrant workers took were notorious for spectacular road accidents and they always came upon one or two. They stared in quick horror at the injured people and their ruined belongings and cars stranded in spoiled heaps along the side of the road. When she and Atilla were younger they had slept in the van overnight but in recent years they'd stopped at motels on the motorways, but it never made going home much fun.

Most of the other Turkish families returning to Europe left about the same time and soon the beach was very quiet. There were tourists, of course, but they were further round the bay and usually stayed on their own beaches. Now a few hesitant groups of local Turkish families appeared. They were the children and relatives of the people who would caretake the holiday homes until the next year's invasion. Apart from the doctor's family from the next door villa, who would be returning to Ankara shortly, Elif knew no one, and when they left she was completely on her own, apart from Atilla.

One morning, when she went down to the beach it was windier than usual. The accustomed calm of the bay was disturbed by uneasy waves, like fur stroked the wrong way. She weighted her towel down with two stones then waded into the sea. If the season was changing she might as well enjoy a decent swim while she could. Further out somebody was using jet-skis. She watched them roar over to the far side of Taşlı Ada. It would be a tourist: there had been loads of them this summer. Most seemed to be from

Germany and France, but quite a few were from England. In previous years Elif and Atilla had enjoyed eavesdropping on their conversations then making some casual remark to each other in their own perfect English. The tourists would be pretty surprised, especially as Elif and Atilla had both looked typically Turkish when they were younger. It had been particularly fun when they detected someone saying something rude about Turkey or Turkish people. They hadn't played the game this year. Atilla, with his long, bleached hair and his earrings could have been a foreigner and Elif hadn't wanted to continue the deception. It had seemed childish.

Now she only wanted to blend into her background and to belong.

The skier reappeared, slicing a widening 'V' out of the bay. The wash slapped against Elif's stomach. Shivering, she lifted her arms above her head, and for the first time, hesitated before diving in. The skier waved. Maybe they thought she'd waved first. It was now or never. She ducked under and came up gasping, shaking her head from side to side, trying to flick her hair out of her eyes. She would only swim as far as the sandbank.

'Hi there,' the skier had switched off the engine and was drifting close by. 'I'm glad I noticed you,' he said. 'They told me in the hotel that it was safer over this side, that there wouldn't be many people swimming.'

'There aren't.'

'But you're here.'

'I'm . . . I'm only local. That's my house, well, my sister's house. We always swim here.'

He bobbed closer and she saw that he was young.

'Was it you who waved the other day?' he asked. 'When we had the yacht?'

'Yes. But I didn't wave today. I just put my arms up.'

'Right.'

She was treading water, wondering what to do next.

'Where did you learn your English?' It was what people always asked.

'In London. Look, I really do have to go.'

Even as she spoke, she couldn't think why she'd said that. There was nobody up at the house. If she wanted to, she could have chatted to him for hours. Then she could say goodbye. That's what she would have done in England. Why was she acting differently, now that she was here?

'E – lif! Elif? Come here!' Atilla's voice rang out. She felt herself reddening with irritation.

'See you then,' the tourist turned the key in the ignition and the jet-ski began to move. When it was a safe distance he waved, then opened the throttle up and raced back towards the island.

'Just what do you think you're doing?' Atilla was kicking at sand on the beach.

'What the hell do you mean?' She was so furious. 'Don't play the big macho brother with me, you . . . you toddler!' Actually he was taller than she was. He had shot up recently and it had surprised them both. For all the rest of their lives she would be shorter than him. Now he laughed at her scornfully.

'Oh, *that's* it, is it? Fancied him, did you? Well, don't let me stop you. I don't want to cramp your style.'

'Then what *do* you want?'

'Nothing.'

'Oh for crying out loud!' She ducked under the water again. It was warmer in than out. Maybe she'd swim off, well past the sandbank.

'Don't go, Eli,' he begged. 'Don't leave me on my own.'

32

'Why not?'

'I'm scared.' He was digging one toe down into the sand, not looking at her. 'They might still come.'

'Who might?'

'Those bullies. The ones from school. They frighten me, Elif. I don't know what to do. I keep thinking about it. Supposing they were on that yacht, supposing they're out here, looking for me ... What'd I do, Elif?'

'Is that why you didn't want me to talk to that bloke?'

'Yes. He might *be* one of them, mightn't he?'

'One of *who*?'

'Them! The ones who said they'd get me! That's *who*!' he was yelling at her as though she were the enemy.

The jet-ski screamed its way around another loop. This time she didn't wave. Atilla's shoulders shook. He sniffed and wiped his nose like a kid. Up at the house the shutters remained closed. There was already an appearance of neglect that she did not like.

'Where's Hatice Teyze? she asked.

'How should I know? Why?'

'It's just that she hasn't opened up. I wondered if she'd gone somewhere.'

He looked round anxiously.

'I bet she has, the lazy pig. I bet she's gone and left us. On purpose. So that they can come and get me.' His voice was shrill with self pity.

'Don't be so stupid, Ati. There's nobody here. This is just ... just ...'

But she didn't know what it was and it frightened her. She pulled her towel free of the stones and put it round his shoulders and then, shivering herself, propelled him towards the house.

Hatice Teyze's grandson, Noyan, was sitting on the

swing with a look of immense satisfaction on his face. In one hand he held the remains of a simit, a bread ring coated with toasted sesame seeds. He had bitten neatly all around the outer edge. He smiled at them shyly and Elif realized that she'd hadn't seen him on the swing all summer. Her sister's boys were always fighting over it and he had stood to one side, waiting to be allowed to push. She ruffled his hair gently as they passed and he held out the rest of the simit.

'No, honestly. You have it. Is Hatice Teyze in the house?'

His mouth was full but he nodded vigorously.

'See?' she said to Atilla, hoping to reassure him, but he scowled disagreeably.

'She's just a lazy bitch, like the rest of them: as soon as Refik Abi goes and isn't keeping watch, they put their feet up. Typical!'

She was too appalled to reply, and they went round the back towards the kitchen in miserable silence.

Hatice Teyze stood by the cooker dropping handfuls of home-made macaroni into a saucepan of boiling water. She was a short, thick-set woman with her grey hair tied up in a coloured muslin scarf. Her hands always moved quickly while the rest of her seemed calm and at ease. She turned towards them now, holding out a few of the tiny uncooked squares. When they were little it had been a treat to be allowed to nibble the uncooked dough. It was a beautiful golden colour and still tasted of the wheat that grew in the fields around Hatice Teyze's village. Neither of them had ever forgotten the afternoon when they'd disregarded her advice to 'only eat a few'. They'd stolen handfuls and eaten it secretly. Later, when it had swelled in their stomachs, they'd cried pathetically with the pain. Hatice Teyze hadn't been cross, but had sat up with them and rubbed their

34

tummies with cotton wool soaked in lemon cologne. In all these years Hatice Teyze had barely changed: she still treated them as children.

'Here,' she encouraged, 'but not too many: you know what can happen.'

The kitchen smelt strongly of garlic. Hatice Teyze had been pounding it into the yoghurt which they would pour on top. It made Elif feel hungry, and she hurried in. Then she saw that Hatice Teyze was not alone. There were four or five men gathered around the table with Ahmet Efendi. The litter of a meal lay before them: bread cut into thick slices, crumbs of white cheese and the rinds of melon. One of them picked up his glass and drained it; another folded away a newspaper. Elif sensed that she had interrupted something, that their conversation had been broken off like a snapped stick when she entered. One of them shuffled together several sheets of typed paper and put them quickly back in a folder. They were strangers, but almost certainly Turks.

'Here,' Hatice Teyze took the towel from Atilla and handed it to Elif. 'Here, my dear, you'll catch your death!' She draped it around her and held her close, rubbing her arms and blotting her wet hair. It was only then, from the comfortable warmth of Hatice Teyze's embrace that Elif realized that she had been standing dripping wet in the crowded kitchen, wearing only a small, bright red bikini.

4

A Moth at Night

A few days later a heatwave of enormous intensity sank down over the bay. Elif woke in the night desperate for a drink of water. Her mouth and eyelids were swollen. The palms of her hands were puffy as if she had rubbed them raw with hard work. She hadn't, of course. During the previous week she'd done nothing at all. Now she slowly sat up in bed and tried to swallow with a dry throat. The air was thick and close. She could even smell her own sweat. Her watch registered 3.20 a.m.

She felt her way downstairs on hot, bare feet and didn't click the light on until she was in the kitchen. Then she jumped back: the floor was alive with cockroaches. There were even some on the patterned oilcloth on the table. Others were on the shelves. She could hear their frail, barbed legs scratching and clinging as they scuttled back into the night-time corners. She knew that there were cockroaches in the house but always forgot about them during the day. Each time she caught sight of them she was disgusted anew. Now she stepped quickly into one of the pairs of slippers which Hatice Teyze kept in the kitchen for her visitors. A big earthenware testi holding drinking water stood near the back door. Elif lifted off the cloth and was so thirsty that she could have gulped the water straight from the ladle, but she didn't and took a glass from one of the narrow shelves.

It was such an old-fashioned kitchen. Although Refik

36

Bey had built on to the front of his house, where it faced the sea, and had made it very modern, the old part at the back, where the kitchen was, had hardly changed. Out under the balcony there was an electric barbecue from America; here Sevim and Hatice Teyze still cooked on two gas rings attached to a battered cylinder of liquid gas. It looked dangerous and Filiz Hanım always worried about the danger of explosions. Elif didn't worry about that, but was surprised that her sister, who spent so much of her life in the kitchen, should put up with such primitive conditions. There was no microwave or deep freeze. Sevim only shrugged her drooping shoulders and said, 'That's Turkey for you.' But it wasn't true. Other summer houses had been modernized and were better equipped than Elif's home in England. Even Hatice Teyze joked that in her village her kitchen was better than this. Her sons had brought everything from Germany. She wouldn't be without it, she said.

No, this wasn't just Turkey, this was Refik Bey's house, and Sevim just seemed to have accepted it. Nothing in this kitchen had been changed for years. Even the shelving around the walls was the original, made from strips of painted wood and so narrow that glasses only just had room. Plates had to be stood up and angled, one over-lapping another, like a pile that has tipped. The shelves were lined with strips of material edged with handmade lace. Such homes were usually seen in villages or shanty towns. It was hardly the kitchen of a 'real Istanbul girl'. Presumably Sevim's house and kitchen in the city were the real thing. Elif suspected that her sister didn't care about this house: that was why she neglected it.

She replaced the glass and smoothed back the lace. As she did so something pricked her finger. She licked off the

37

blob of blood and felt along the shelf under the glasses. Yes, there was something. Somebody had cut something out of a newspaper and pinned it there, underneath the material. It hadn't been done recently either, because the pin had already rusted through onto the cloth.

Elif dislodged something else. It fluttered from its hiding place: a neatly cut corner of cardboard with a name, 'Ferhat', printed on in blue biro, with a number below. She glanced at the article. It was only about cotton farming in the South and there wasn't even a photo. Puzzled, Elif put them both back, exactly as she'd found them. Hatice Teyze couldn't read, so they were unlikely to be hers. They probably weren't anybody's, or even of interest at all, not now. They couldn't be important if they had been forgotten, rusting away under the glasses. Still, maybe she shouldn't have looked. It wasn't her home and she had no right to pry.

Yet there was something about the kitchen. Some atmosphere, or maybe just some bad smell, pervaded it. Was it a minute trace of escaping gas, as her mother always feared, or drains? When Hatice Teyze washed the floor she threw buckets of soapy water over the tiles, then brushed the suds away through a hole in the wall. The dirty water was supposed to run straight out into drains in the garden, but they were often blocked so it trickled back and a small, scummy pool was left slowly evaporating in the midday sun. That must be it.

And it was so hot and so still. The day, when it came, would be scorching. Outside a large moth, attracted to the light, flew repeatedly against the wire mesh over the window. Yes, the kitchen definitely stank. Above the everyday smells of food and spices, of mint cut through and parsley chopped and of tarhana, the dried, peppery soup which was stored in a cotton bag hung from a nail, there was this other unpleasant odour.

Elif plunged the ladle in deeper and drank again but wasn't refreshed. It was so hot that the water from the testi was barely cool. The kitchen was airless. The perspiration on her body hadn't dried at all. The moth drummed against the wire as though it could get through in the end. Elif put her hand on the key but the back door was unlocked. Pushing it open she stepped into the night.

Outside the heat was overwhelming. It was all around her and when she touched the outside wall, she could feel it deep within, stored up, over all the long years of summers. The dusty, white-washed stones were as warm as animal skin. Above the bay, a sliver of crescent moon, like a thinly pared rind of lemon, hung in the night sky. It was absolutely quiet. Nothing moved along the coast road and even the sea was still. Previously she had always been aware of some edge of breeze blowing onto the shore or she had caught the slap of water under the black rocks. Tonight the velvet movement of the sea was imperceptible beneath the moon.

She could have slept out here in the garden. She lifted her damp hair away from the nape of her neck: she must cut it shorter. It was too heavy for this heat. The moth, drawn to the brighter wedge of light around the door, left the wire and flew into her face. She knocked it away but it caught and tangled amongst her hair. Horrified, she felt it against her mouth and tasted its dust on her lips and tongue. She wanted to be rid of it, but felt its fluttering wings all over her.

'Mujde!' Someone else was out there too, 'Good news', they said.

'Mujde,' a man's voice repeated softly, 'don't be afraid, a

moth is a bearer of news. That's what we say: that the one touched by a moth will soon hear news. Good news, İnşallah.'

He was right, but she still wanted to escape.

'Who's there?' It was an unfamiliar voice. 'Who is it?' She had retreated to the lighted doorway, her heart pounding.

'I'm . . . I'm a grandson of Ahmet Efendi, from his village. I'm sorry. I know I've frightened you.'

'No you haven't. It was only the moth.' She could make him out now: a man in a white shirt, sitting on the low wall under the lemon tree. He got up.

'Shall I catch it now? Shall I catch the moth for you, if it's frightening you?'

It was a young man's voice and Elif guessed from the sound of it that he was smiling. From the safety of the night he was laughing at her foolishness. She didn't know what to say. Then, from the room beside the kitchen, where Hatice Teyze and Ahmet Efendi and Noyan slept, someone stirred. They turned over, muttered in their sleep and began to snore loudly, each laboured breath ending in a ridiculous, high-pitched whine.

'Sounds like my grandfather,' the man said.

Elif began to giggle.

'Well,' he said tentatively, 'it doesn't sound as though the heat's spoiling his sleep.'

'No . . .' She couldn't say any more. Her laughter spilled into the night and she heard him begin to laugh too. Then he said, 'Goodnight,' and turned away. Glancing sideways, she made out a blanket folded over the wooden bench outside the kitchen door. So he had been sleeping there, under the crescent moon.

This was where she and Atilla had taken afternoon rests

when they were little. In fact, it was where Hatice Teyze did a lot of her work. She'd sit cross-legged, cleaning trays of rice and dried beans, picking over basins of spinach and sewing the clean sheets onto quilts. In the evenings, after the day's work was done, she'd sit there again and knit amazingly complicated clothes for her various grand-children. She'd knitted things for Elif, but she'd never worn them. They hadn't looked right in England. Sometimes Hatice Teyze entertained visitors from her village. Then she'd ply them with tea and newly bought biscuits, and they'd gossip for hours. When she was younger Elif had always joined in. The women fussed over her, joking about her accent and her inaccurate Turkish. They teased her about her boyish figure and behaviour. They called her 'küçük İngiliz', 'the little English one', and asked her about Princess Diana and whether the English wore shoes in their houses and were as dirty as people said. Now that Turkey was to be her home Elif realized that she could join them on equal terms.

She slept late, and when she went into the garden there was no trace of the visitor. Hatice Teyze was sitting on the bench threading a length of cotton through the stems of a heap of peppers. The needle flashed in the sun and Elif saw that one of the walls was already covered with rows of peppers, hung up to dry. They reminded her of chunky modern necklaces which had been fashionable in England a year or so ago. Noyan was squatting nearby, helping his grandmother.

'Shall I do some too?' Elif offered.

'If you like, but there isn't another needle. Except Noyan's.'

'OK.' Elif held out her hand and smiled. The little boy looked beseechingly at his grandma, then finding no

41

response, relinquished his needle. Elif saw his disappointment and felt guilty.

'Look, *you* do them, Noyan. Or we could take turns,' she offered. He shook his head miserably and wandered away.

'What's the matter with him?' she asked when the child was out of earshot. He had reminded her of her own brother.

'Nothing! What *should* be the matter with him?' asked Hatice Teyze briskly.

'He doesn't *say* much, does he?'

'What can he say? He's homesick, for Germany! And he's under my feet.'

They worked on in silence. The child fiddled with something in the dust, and rubbed his fists into his eyes. Elif had seen Atilla do that. He had always been on the edge of things in the school playground. In primary school Elif had kept an eye on him, waiting for him at the end of school and letting him play with her girl-friends at breaktime. He'd been so sweet then. The others had pulled him onto their laps, stroking his fair hair and kissing him extravagantly. When her parents had let her have a sleepover party for her eleventh birthday, he had been allowed in the room too, as a sort of honorary girl. He had been such a lamb. He wasn't one of those beastly little brothers who spied on their sisters through the bathroom keyhole. Atilla had been different. When Elif went to secondary school things had changed. She still dropped him off at the school gates and picked him up in the afternoons, but he was always alone: a slight, golden-haired boy, who sniffed back tears and did nothing when other children kicked his school bag into puddles in the playground and took his money and his lunch from him. He drifted through the day, always late for lessons, always losing his games kit or his books and sometimes not turning up at all. A few people, teachers mainly, said that he was a useless, spoiled brat. Her father once said that it was Elif's fault, that she'd taken away his confidence by fussing over him so absurdly. But it wasn't true. If she hadn't taken care of him, he would never have survived.

Now, carefully pulling the thread through the stem, Elif wondered what she should do about school here. Her mother had reminded her on the phone last night, and assumed that Refik Bey would be arranging something in Istanbul. The phone call had upset Elif: her friend Claire had been round to the house and was *so* surprised and then quite off-hand when she heard that Elif wasn't coming home. Later, her mother had seen Miss Baverstock, who took maths, in the supermarket, but she'd managed to avoid her and get away without being recognized. 'I mean,' her mother's cheerful voice had echoed down the line, 'I wouldn't have known *what* to say to *her*. She'd never understand!' It was true. Everyone was scared of Miss Baverstock. She was a tiny, black-eyed Scot who did the rounds of pubs and arcades, hauling her truanting pupils out by their shirt-tails. Elif struggled with maths, but Miss Baverstock had assured her that she could get a decent grade in the exam. She'd even said that Emma Risdale would pass, and Emma Risdale had been planning to fail everything so that she wouldn't have to go into the sixth form. Miss Baverstock would be disappointed by Elif's failure to return.

Listening to her mother, Elif was acutely aware that her life in England was over. The endless grey afternoons that were never as bright as one had hoped in the morning, and the miserable Monday lunch-times when other people talked about what they'd done at the weekends, were in the past. Elif never did much at weekends so she had nothing to tell. All she'd done was dance near Frankie at the Saturday disco. She'd fancied Frankie ever since they'd both been about twelve and the teacher had made him sit beside her. It had been a punishment for Frankie to sit by a goody-goody like Elif. She hadn't spoken a word to him, but had nearly died of excitement. Now, people said that he was going out with some really young girl from the estates, but whenever Elif saw him he was still with a crowd of mates. She couldn't believe that all that was over for ever.

They finished the last of the peppers and tied them in place against the wall. Brushing the hair out of her face, Elif felt a burning sensation: she had touched her eyes with fingers stained with pepper juice. When she tried to wipe it away she made it worse and suddenly tears were streaming down her face. Hatice Teyze laughed and sent her in to wash her face and hands. From the patch of shade by the rubbish bins, Noyan looked up and smiled with satisfaction.

Atilla got up in time for lunch. Creases from the pillow were still pressed into his cheek and his hair dripped where he'd stood under the shower. Elif stroked it as she went past but he jerked his head away, yelling at her to get off. He ate greedily, stuffing himself with köfte and not bothering to look to see if there were enough meatballs to go round. She hated it when he was like that. Hopefully it was because he was thirteen; if so, she only had to wait. When her mother asked about him on the phone Elif always said that he was fine, but now she wasn't so sure. Sometimes she was afraid that the terror he had displayed on the beach had been caused by more than classroom bullies who mocked him as 'Atilla the Ant'.

Hatice Teyze brought an enormous watermelon to the

table. She sawed a circle from the base and top, then up-ended it and thrust the point of the knife into the centre. The red flesh split with a tearing sound and a pool of juice ran out onto the oilcloth. Noyan picked up his slice and nibbled at it awkwardly, trying to stop the liquid running down his chin.

'Poor little one,' his grandmother made sympathetic noises. 'He doesn't even know how to eat properly. Over there, in Germany, they don't have watermelons. All their fruit is in tins!' She took the slice from him and chopped it up into neat pieces.

'There. Now you can enjoy it, you little German!'

'I don't like it,' he said quietly.

'Don't like watermelon?' Hatice Teyze was puzzled. 'But everybody likes watermelon! Now eat up and don't be a donkey!' She was gathering the large black pips onto a plate; later she would roast them with salt.

'It's different, over there,' muttered Atilla. 'They have different fruits too.'

'That's right,' shouted Noyan triumphantly, 'and they aren't in tins.'

'Well, they may not be in tins, but they won't be as fresh as this!' Hatice Teyze was determined not be to outdone. She went over to the sink and began washing up noisily. She sighed heavily.

'Shall we help?' asked Elif. She had an unpleasant sense of being a burden.

'No, no. It's *my* job. That's what Refik Bey pays me for. And anyway, that one wouldn't know how to help,' she nodded at Atilla.

'Of course he knows how! He has to help at home!' Irritated, Elif held the sponge out to Atilla but he laughed in her face and pushed past her into the garden, hissing in

English, 'Well, we're not at home now, are we, big sister?'

Noyan scrambled from his chair and ran after the new hero. Ahmet Efendi watched them go, then lit a cigarette and shook his head slowly. Hatice Teyze plunged her hands into the steaming water.

Then the telephone rang. Elif hurried to answer it. Refik Bey was calling from Bursa. He was sorry not to have called them before, he'd been too busy. He hadn't forgotten about them, not for one minute. He'd be coming to get them any day now. Was she all right? And Atilla?

'Refik Abi . . . about school?'

'All in good time, Elif,' he said pleasantly. Then he asked for Ahmet Efendi to come to the phone. There were orders to be given, about preparing the house for winter.

It was two weeks before he called again. By then the autumn heatwave had waned and the bay was quieter than ever. Elif began letters to Emma and Claire but she put them aside: nothing had happened that she could write about.

5

On the Swing

One morning the tranquillity of the bay was disturbed by shrieks of laughter. Days had rolled by with no sign of Refik Bey. Hatice Teyze was tired of waiting. She had begun to close up the house. The silk carpets had been beaten and wiped. Now she was rolling them up in old sheets. Soon they would be locked away in one of the smaller rooms. The furniture had been cleaned and covered with dust sheets and the whole house reeked of naphthalene and furniture polish. Elif had helped, spending hours on her hands and knees rubbing wax into the already perfect wooden floor in the guest rooms. At the sound of this laughter, she got up stiffly and looked out. Noyan was laughing.

Hatice Teyze had worked her way through the house. Only the kitchen and their room beyond were left, apart from the two rooms which Elif and Atilla occupied. Elif knew that she was in the way and that it wasn't only Noyan who got under Hatice Teyze's feet. Each autumn Hatice Teyze returned to her village and this year she would be taking this grandson. She would stay through the planting season and on until the school year finished in early summer next year. Ahmet Efendi always remained alone in the house as its caretaker. Elif knew that their unexpected presence was holding everything up. Hatice Teyze had denied it, but Ahmet Efendi had nodded when she'd mentioned it.

'Yes,' he agreed, over supper, 'it has made some

difficulties. And I'm afraid it'll make some more, before we're through.'

'Why?' Atilla had asked, indignantly. 'We'll be gone as soon as we can! And anyway, we'd much rather be in Istanbul.'

'Maybe – ' Ahmet Efendi fell silent. He crumbled bread into the tarhana soup and scattered on another pinch of red pepper before beginning to eat. The next morning Elif had cleared the belongings from both their rooms down into the hall. They would sleep on the divans there, she said, or even outside, until Refik Bey came. She wasn't going to be in anybody's way. Atilla had protested, then forgotten about it. He had found a new friend. It was their laughter which drew Elif to the window.

In the garden the older boy was with Noyan. After that conversation about fruit the two had become inseparable. Noyan followed Atilla around like a shadow and Atilla clearly enjoyed being his hero. Now Elif watched them fooling about with the swing. Noyan was standing up on it, clinging tightly to the chains, with his bare toes curled over the edge of the seat. Atilla, standing behind, was pushing him wildly, higher and higher. Each time the swing fell back from the top of its arc, Noyan shrieked with terrified laughter. Straight away, as soon as the momentum slackened and he could catch his breath, he begged for more. Atilla crouched like a wild cat, waiting to spring. He pushed with all the strength he possessed and seemed oblivious to the danger.

Elif called out but neither took any notice. She hurried downstairs, determined to prevent an accident. Her brother had always been reckless. She'd lost count of the number of times she'd 'saved him'. He'd climbed too high in a neighbour's tree and then got stuck, frozen and mute with

48

fear in the topmost branches. She'd helped him down, step by step, with a hand clenched around each ankle. He'd jumped into the deep end of the swimming pool long before he could swim, and then the winter before last he'd walked out over thin ice on the pond in the park. It hadn't been Elif who had rescued him that time. A passing jogger had heard Atilla's cries and crawled out on his stomach to drag him clear. When the boy was safe, this man had shouted at Elif for not looking after her little brother properly. It hadn't been fair because Atilla wasn't 'little' at all, not then. He'd been in secondary school, though he'd probably appeared younger. He always had, until recently. Lately he'd grown so tall.

Elif never told her parents about these narrow escapes. She hadn't wanted to worry them. They had always had so much to do, often leaving home for the workshop while it was dark and only returning late into the night. When they'd opened the shop they'd worked even harder. They always said that they couldn't have done it without Elif's help: she was such a mature, sensible girl. She could never have let them down and told them that their only son was in trouble. Sometimes, despite all her efforts, news did filter home. The small Turkish community was expert in passing gossip around. Somebody told them that Atilla was shoplifting and they had been appalled. Luckily it had only been temporary: Atilla had got in with a bad crowd. Their father had thrashed him so severely that he hadn't gone to school for a couple of days. After that Elif had tried to take even better care of him.

'Don't!' she shouted at Atilla, running towards the swing. 'Be careful!'

Noyan twisted his head round in surprise. Atilla missed his stroke and pushed crookedly. Noyan screamed and

slipped forward. As the swing hit the post, he fell off. It
flew out once more, the chains jangling as though alive,
until Elif caught hold of them and brought it to a halt.
Noyan's face was covered in blood.

'You fool!' Atilla screamed. 'Look what you've made me
do! You made me kill him!'

For a moment Elif thought that he was going to hit her.

'You haven't killed me,' said Noyan thickly. More blood
from his split lip ran down between his fingers.

'See?' snarled Atilla. 'You *almost* killed him. Why can't
you leave me alone, Elif? You always ruin everything! Why
don't you just *go away*? You spoil my fun.'

'Fun,' protested Elif. 'You call that *fun*?'

Noyan, who was bleeding all over his T-shirt, regarded
them from under smeared brows.

'It *was* fun,' he protested loyally. He and Atilla exchanged
guilty grins before making their way, arm in arm, towards
the beach, like wounded soldiers retreating from the enemy.

She almost followed, wanting to make it up. After all,
Atilla never meant to upset her. She was sure of that. He
just said idiotic things, especially when he was frightened.
And Noyan could have been badly hurt. It was luck that
he'd only cut his lip. Maybe Atilla was right: if she hadn't
interfered that wouldn't have happened.

'Come *on*,' Atilla shouted as Noyan lagged behind. 'Be
quick, or she'll catch us.' Then she heard the sound of
someone trying to loosen Ahmet Efendi's boat from its
blocks.

'Hurry!' Atilla urged, but there was no need. Elif was
already walking towards the coast road.

On the bus into town she pushed her way through to a
vacant seat then surreptitiously counted the money in her
purse. It was lucky that she hadn't bought presents for the

girls in England. Hopefully she still had enough for two coach tickets to Istanbul. She'd been thinking about this for several days. Suddenly she wanted to leave at once.

They needn't wait for Refik Bey and there was no reason why she shouldn't make that decision. She had always made decisions in England. Her parents had been pleased. 'It's your life,' they said, 'you can do as you want.' Friends had envied her and had been surprised at her independence because Turkish parents were expected to be stricter than English ones. Elif had explained that this had never been a problem for her. Luckily, she hadn't wanted to stay out all night or do things that she knew her parents would disapprove of, so there hadn't been much scope for disagreements. Her parents were away so much that someone had to be home to look after Atilla, and that person had always been her.

It might have been different if her parents had been like Emma's. They were both unemployed and sat around the house getting on each other's nerves. The main event in their day was Emma's return from school. They pounced on her as soon as she dropped her rucksack in the hall: 'What sort of a day did you have, darling? Have you got homework? What do you want for your tea? Did you do OK in that maths test your dad helped you with?' Poor Emma. Elif, who was used to managing on her own, found this concern overwhelming. Emma did too. No wonder she was determined to leave school as soon as she could. No, there really wasn't a problem. She'd buy two coach tickets for the next day, and that would be that. She could phone Sevim that evening.

The bus slowed down at the bend below the castle and suddenly there it was: bazaar day with stalls and carts spilling out of the marketplace and along the road. She had forgotten that this was Friday. No wonder the bus was so crowded. Other passengers were on their feet, pushing to get off. They carried her with them, a bright crowd of comfortable housewives, with only a man or two amongst them. Their heavy, gold bangles chinked as they grabbed the rails to steady themselves. Even in this hot weather they were fully clothed in thick stockings and hand-knitted sleeveless waistcoats. Firmly gripping shopping bags and the odd child, they made for the bazaar with that small-stepped, unhurried walk of Turkish women. Never, Elif reflected, did women run, unless it was someone very young or for sport. Yet they were endlessly busy and hardworking. They never stamped along the pavements in ringing high heels as they did in England, nor shouted with laughter in the streets. It was a gentler way of life here and to Elif it was very attractive.

She watched the women bending over golden-green piles of grapefruits, following the seller's darting hands to make sure that he only put sound fruit on the scales. They were experts and knew all the tricks of the bazaar. Elif loved shopping out of doors. There, chickpeas were roasting over a charcoal burner, here, someone had sliced open blood oranges. He was squeezing their dark juice into a glass. 'Wine!' he cried. 'Like wine, only sweeter and cheaper!' He held it out to them, one after another, but they all smiled and passed him by. When he offered the glass to Elif, she copied the others, tossing her head back indifferently, even though the sight and scent of the juice had made the saliva run in her mouth. If they hadn't been leaving, she would have bought some oranges.

She wandered past the fish stalls where the catch was laid out on round, red trays like the petals of huge, silver flowers. The fishermen shouted the names of the fish and flung water on them with hands stained with blood and glistening with scales. She loved fish. It was such a shame that Ahmet Efendi hadn't taken them to the island. Now it was too late. She remembered how they had sat on the rocks, watching the mottled skins blister and char. The coarse grains of salt that Hatice Teyze had rubbed into the flesh had crunched between their teeth and tasted powerfully of the sea. They had pulled out the backbones and tossed them aside, before splitting open the crusts of newly baked bread and laying in the steaming pieces of fish. They'd made a salad with lettuce and long fronds of parsley. The spring onions from Ahmet Efendi's garden had been as sweet as sugar. Maybe next year . . .

'Spinach! Fresh spinach!' A little boy with a voice hoarse from years of shouting stood between older men. 'Spinach!' he growled again. 'As smart as an MP's new suit! Fresh spinach for sale!' When she glanced at the mound lying on the tarpaulin at their feet, she saw that he was telling the truth. The leaves were uncrushed and the curving stems were as soft and pink as the edges of clouds.

Sevim made wonderful spinach pie. When they got to Istanbul she'd ask her sister to make one for them to celebrate their arrival. Sevim would be flattered and delighted, wouldn't she? For one awkward moment, Elif remembered that she'd never been in her sister's Istanbul house. Once, on the journey back to England, she'd waited outside in the van while her father had hurried indoors to collect something. She had been younger then and could only remember that the house had been up a side street in one of the old parts of the town. It had looked very old itself, with carved wooden balconies and rather garish paint in different shades of green. There was a well in the front garden and Atilla had wanted to investigate but she'd held him back because wells are dangerous. He'd scratched her, but she had held on. That house had been near the sea too, though the Bosphorus, joining the Black Sea to the Mediterranean, was more like a wide river than a sea. Still, it would be wonderful to be there, especially in spring and summer; and by next summer, it would feel like home.

She paused to watch people buying dried goods from one stall. It was very popular. The men selling were deftly filling brown paper bags with lentils and dried beans and streams of pearly rice. There were sacks of dried apricots and black cherries and the white mulberries, which always reminded Elif of caterpillars so that she could never eat them. Mint, sage and camomile stood near sacks full of nuts and dates and ground henna. That was another thing which she could enjoy here: she'd dye her hair. She'd never dared in England, because she was afraid of looking different. Here it wouldn't matter; all sorts of people hennaed their hair, even old women and men. She'd cut hers first, then henna it. She paused by the sack of green powder and was just going to dip her finger into it, when somebody said, 'Hello again.'

It was one of the young men who was selling. He paused, with a scoop of dried figs swinging on the scales and smiled at her before dropping on another one, to make up the weight.

'Don't you recognize me?'

'No.' But she did.

'I'm Yaşar.' He quickly folded over the open end before bending in the corners. He took the money and handed back change, but watched her all the time.

'I'm Ahmet Efendi's relative, well, grandson, actually. I'm Yaşar. We met that hot night. In your garden.'

That, of course, was what she had recognized. It was the

54

sound of his voice. But she still didn't know what to say to him.

'Did you want some of this?' he was pointing to the henna.

'No,' she shook her head. 'Not really.' Behind her someone grumbled and she was aware that she had jumped the queue.

'No? Not just a tiny little bit?' Was he laughing at her, again?

'No. Anyway, I'm going away. To Istanbul.'

'To Istanbul? We've got a shop there. Maybe – '

'When you have a moment, young man,' a woman elbowed Elif aside, 'I'll have three kilos of chickpeas.'

He dug a scoop into the sack and the peas rattled into the bag like summer hail.

Then someone called out.

'Ferhat Abi! Is Ferhat Abi around?' A young boy, dressed in the white shirt and black şalvar of the countryside pushed his way through the crowd. He was balancing a tray of simit on a ring of cloth on his head. 'Ferhat Abi?' he called again. From the back of the stall, a tall man with immensely dark eyes and a neat line of black moustache, looked up from the pile of sacks which he had been quietly mending.

'Who is asking for Ferhat Abi?' he said.

'I am,' replied the boy. 'I've brought his simit, and some news.' He swung the tray from his head and set it on its stand, then chose a simit with care and handed it over. He also gave an envelope to the man called Ferhat. Then he put the tray back on his head, slung the stand over his shoulder and disappeared into the crowd. Elif noticed that he hadn't taken any money. Even when she could no longer see him she could still hear his shrill, breaking voice, 'Simit for sale. Fresh simit.'

'Here.'

She turned quickly: someone had touched her arm. Yaşar was holding a small bag towards her.

'I can't take it,' she said awkwardly, anxious that she couldn't pay him and still have enough for the tickets.

'Why not? Aren't we relatives, well, almost?' He was smiling persuasively. 'Take it for your journey. This journey to Istanbul. Please, take it.' Surely there was some slight accent in his speech?

'All right. Thank you.' He might have dropped it into the dust if she hadn't agreed. When she looked back Yaşar was serving someone else. The man called Ferhat had opened the envelope and was reading intently.

The coach tickets were more expensive than she had expected but she just had enough. Constant price rises were one of the things that always surprised her about Turkey. Things became more expensive from week to week. Everybody complained, but it still went on and Elif never got used to it. She hesitated and looked across at the people queuing outside the office of a cheaper coach company. If she bought there she would have money over for food on the way. Then she noticed foreigners queuing with the Turks. They were young, bare-legged men and women in shorts and T-shirts and bowed under enormous rucksacks. One wore no shoes and stood there in all the filth of the coach station. Her face and shoulders were crimson and peeling from too much sun; a vest top revealed the bunch of hairs under her arms. Other people stared too. These were typical 'hippy' tourists, the sort of people her parents always made fun of. Unexpectedly, Elif found herself disapproving too. She turned back and bought the more expensive tickets. She didn't want to be anywhere near such foreigners in case people wondered if she too was secretly like that and not a proper Turk at all.

When Elif returned, Hatice Teyze was sitting outside on the wooden bench knitting. Her short, plump legs stuck straight out in front of her and she was wearing patched nylon socks. Noyan sprawled across her, his head in her lap, as though he were still a baby. Their empty tea glasses stood on a tin tray on the ground. The scent of the lemon tree must have made them drowsy.

'Is there any tea left?' Elif asked. She wanted to join them and sit close when she broke the news.

'There is tea,' Hatice Teyze yawned, 'but I won't drink any.' She did not invite Elif to sit down.

'I'll drink,' said Noyan waking up, 'with four sugars, Elif Abla.'

'No, you won't!' Hatice Teyze slapped his bare leg. It wasn't particularly hard but he was quiet, instantly, as though he deserved it.

'Where's Atilla?' Elif asked, and in the moment of silence she knew that something had happened while she was out. Noyan pulled the knitting down so that it hid his face.

'I've bought tickets, Hatice Teyze, for Atilla and me. We can go to Istanbul tomorrow.'

She expected the old woman to protest, to tell her that she shouldn't have done it and that they were welcome to stay as long as they wanted, but she didn't. She sighed, disentangled her work from Noyan who had dug his fingers in and knitted silently to the end of the row.

'Well,' she said coolly, 'good luck to you, Elif. May it be for the best.'

An eddy of dust blew across the garden and the rows of dried peppers shivered and rustled against the wall.

'Autumn's come,' said Hatice Teyze in an altered tone. She took the cardigan from her own shoulders and laid it over the child, as though he could possibly have felt cold in that heat.

It was only later, as their coach was approaching the outskirts of Istanbul, that Atilla told her what had happened. He and Noyan had managed to launch Ahmet Efendi's boat but they had forgotten the oars. A tourist saw they were in trouble and raised the alarm and a fishing boat had gone out from the harbour and brought them back safely.

'But you could have been drowned!' cried Elif.

'No way,' he said confidently. 'I can swim that distance easily.'

'But what about Noyan? He can't swim far at all.'

'What about him?' said Atilla. 'I didn't ask him to get in the boat, did I? Anyway, I'm absolutely starving. Didn't Hatice Teyze give us anything else to eat?'

'No.' Then she remembered the little bag of sweets which Yaşar had given her. She handed it to him in silence.

'Wow!' he whooped sarcastically.

It was full of nâne şekeri, the little mints which people always take on journeys. He tipped the contents onto his palm and was trying to cram them all into his mouth at once, when Elif snatched the bag back from him.

'You pig,' she snapped. There were a few left, stuck together at the bottom. She put one in her mouth, pushed the bag into her pocket, then shut her eyes and let the sweet dissolve slowly. Outside, the huge city of Istanbul stretched restlessly beneath an autumn sky.

6

At Home

'Tinker, tailor, soldier – soldier, sailor, rich man, poor man
. . . poor – what's next, Elif Abla?' Elif's elder nephew,
Hakan, looked up from counting the olive stones on his
breakfast plate. He had started the second year in primary
school and as an afternoon student this year, in the second
shift of children to attend, he found the mornings endless.
Hakan was too restless to wait. Elif had tried and failed to
teach him the time on his new watch. She had more success
with English lessons. Now he could repeat several rhymes,
though he had no idea what they meant.

'Beggar man, thief,' she prompted. This morning they
were alone again. The younger boy, Volkan, was still asleep.
Poor Sevim, who was tormented by morning sickness, had
not appeared either.

'What's "beggarmanthief"?' he asked. She began to
explain although he wasn't listening.

He counted on, busily shifting stones from the smaller
pile to the larger. When he'd finished he grabbed another
handful of olives and ate them rapidly, spitting the stones
back onto the plate. He wasn't such a bad kid and she was
grateful to him: on the evening of their arrival he had run
up and flung his arms around her waist. Volkan had hidden
behind his mother in the shadows of the hallway, acting as
though he'd forgotten who she and Atilla were. Hakan was
also the only one who liked her new, short haircut. The
others had pulled horrified faces but he had rubbed his

hands through her spiky black curls and laughed.

Hakan spat out another stone. Elif was amazed at the amount that he ate. He was a stockily built boy, with a vivid, full-lipped face who was already proud of his manly strength. He could not have been more different from how her own brother had been.

Atilla had been such a slip of a boy. Everyone had commented on his fragility as they stroked his fair hair back from his eyes and ignored the anxious stammer which puckered his pale brow. He had always picked at his food, silently chewing on mouthfuls that he could not swallow and trying to catch her eye so that he might leave the table to spit them out in the bathroom. Tactless visitors had wondered aloud if this sickly creature would live to grow up; but he had. And he'd startled them by turning into an outrageously handsome youth. 'Give him a few more years,' women murmured now, patting his arm appreciatively. Only Elif had been unsurprised by the transformation. She had always known that he was special.

'Isn't it time to go yet?' Hakan asked impatiently, shaking the large watch on his wrist. He peered at it in puzzled disappointment when she said, 'No'. His black school overall and stiff white collar hung ready over the back of a chair. He wasn't allowed to put them on too early in case he messed them up. There was a mark for cleanliness in school.

Now he roamed the room restlessly. He was already wearing his new outdoor shoes. Elif hadn't been able to stop him.

'Tinker, tailor, soldier, sailor ... richmanpoorman, beggarmanthief!' He began to run round the table, going faster and faster, thumping each chair with his fist as he passed.

'Ssh – Volkan's still asleep. And your mother.' Elif

grabbed his arm but he pulled away with a powerful jerk which nearly toppled her from her chair.

'Don't, please,' she begged. He laughed cheerfully but continued the thunder of running, and looked back in the hope that she would jump up and give chase. When she didn't he groaned with boredom, then took another slice of bread. Watching her from under thick, black lashes, with a shine of perspiration on his upper lip, he began to spoon on dollops of honey. He resumed the chant, 'Richman poorman, beggar – '

'What's that "beggar" thing again?' He was tilting his head to one side, trying to get in a corner of the overloaded bread. Honey ran down over his chin and fingers.

She tried to explain and wondered if she dared take the food away from him. It wasn't really that she was afraid, not of a kid who was only eight. It was just that she didn't want to annoy him. His penetrating scream would have roused the whole house. When he had forced the last bits into his mouth he licked his hand and then his wrist with the calm efficiency of a cat, cleaning up after a kill.

'Is Ahmet Efendi a thief?' he asked. 'Father says they have nothing.'

'No! It's not like that. Ahmet Efendi is poor.' She was quite shocked. 'He's not a thief, he's a friend.'

'No, he isn't!' Now Hakan looked shocked. 'He's our worker. That's what Father told me. He always calls him "an old thief".' He looked at her curiously. 'Are you working for us, Elif Abla?'

'No. But I'm going to help you – I want to help your mother – that's why I've stayed here, in Turkey.'

'And what about me? Aren't you going to help me?'

'Yes. Of course I am. If you'd like me to.'

'I don't mind,' he shook his watch again. 'Anyway,

61

women have to help men. Father told me. Isn't it time, yet?'

'No. But you could start to get ready, slowly. You could wash your face and clean your teeth.'

He grinned and raced away. It was much too early, but she couldn't think of what else to do. He was so energetic. No wonder poor Sevim was worn out, even without another baby. Maybe she could walk him to school by a different route. They could go down to the park on the waterfront and she could buy him something else to eat. After they'd killed time there, they could come back up to the school. Today, she'd walk slowly with little dainty steps like a Turkish woman.

Elif didn't need to take Hakan to school but it filled a small space in the long autumn day. It was also an excuse to leave the house. For some reason that was unclear, Refik Bey had been unable to arrange a school place for either her or Atilla. He was so busy, he said, and the bureaucracy in schools was dreadful. To make things easier she had suggested that he concentrate on Atilla's school first. She wasn't absolutely sure that she wanted to be back in school, but her brother was different. Refik Bey nodded and praised her sense of family responsibility.

Now, however, when she watched other teenagers hurrying out of their houses on their way to school, she wished she'd kept her mouth shut. She saw them gathering in cafés and ice-cream parlours and lingering in the parks to chat and gossip after school and she felt appallingly lonely. She hadn't spoken to anyone outside the family yet and hadn't been anywhere on her own, apart from her trip to the hairdresser.

It wasn't as if Sevim needed her help, either. Zehra Hanım lived with them in Istanbul and most of the work was done by the Akbulut family who occupied the old guest house in the garden. Elif knew that they were distant relatives, but she had not realized how important they seemed to be. Now she couldn't avoid them. On the evening of her arrival they had knocked on the back door and begged to be introduced, even though it was so late. Zehra Hanım had ushered them in, but they'd hung back shyly. Refusing to approach, they insisted that it was enough of an honour just to peep at the young lady and gentleman from England. They didn't want to intrude on this family reunion, but they just had to say 'welcome' before going back to their own humble home. Ömer Akbulut was a short, middle-aged man with a limp; his wife, Gülfidan was much younger. Zehra Hanım scolded them: Elif and Atilla were nothing special. Then Gülfidan strode across the room and seized Elif's hand. She kissed it and touched it to her forehead before motioning her husband to do the same. He bent over Elif's hand, calling her 'abla', 'elder sister', although he was twenty years older than she was.

The pair had sat on the sofa, side by side, and accepted cologne, a chocolate, then coffee and finally tea. Elif, struggling to suppress her yawns, had hated them instantly and passionately and for no reason at all.

This morning her desire to avoid Gülfidan encouraged her to leave the house early. Wherever she went, this woman appeared. It was as though she lay in wait for Elif. She would suddenly call out, asking yet again if there was anything *else* that she or her husband, Ömer, could do for Elif? Anything at all! They'd do it at once, no matter how busy they were. Once Elif had found her at an open drawer in her bedroom. When she asked her what she was doing, Gülfidan had smiled and said, 'Tidying, of course', and it was true. Elif's clothes had been sorted and refolded in neat, tight piles. Elif had frowned.

63

'Oh, dear,' Gülfidan had apologized extravagantly. 'I can see you're not pleased. I won't do it again. Not if I haven't done it properly. Because of course, I haven't been abroad. Humble people like us don't have that chance, so we don't know any better.'

'It's all right,' Elif had said grudgingly. Gülfidan had glanced over the drawer before shutting it, smiling her own, satisfied smile and left the room with a small shake of her head.

Now, as Elif and Hakan went down the steps towards the front gate, Gülfidan's voice rang out again:

'Hakan? Where are *you* off to?'

'School!' he yelled back.

'Isn't it too early?' Gülfidan acted as if Elif wasn't there.

'No!' Hakan yelled. 'It's the right time!' He brandished his watch. 'Elif Abla said so!'

'Oh! Excuse *me*,' Gülfidan's tone changed to one of apology, 'I didn't see Elif Abla. Of course, that's *quite* different. I expect they tell the time differently in England. Only here, we say it's ten-thirty. And that's too early for school.'

'It *isn't*. You're wrong!' Hakan looked anxiously from one to the other of them, then back at his watch which he shook violently, just in case.

All the way down to the park he grumbled that Elif had made him get ready too early. Now he'd have to wait for hours because nobody else would be out to play. He kicked at things and his pink cheeks became crimson as his sense of outrage grew. He even managed a pathetic sniff as Elif pushed open the park gate. It did not look very inviting. The summer's heat had stunted the grass and autumn's rains had not yet come to revive it. It was empty except for an old woman on one of the benches. A toddler squatted at her feet and played with the dust and stones. A cold breeze blew in off the Bosphorus.

'Go on!' she said to Hakan, giving him a slight push. 'Play!'

'Can't.'

'Why not?'

'There's nobody to play with.' Sulkily he scuffed his shoes against the edge of a flower bed of dead plants.

'Rubbish,' Elif was determined to be unsympathetic. 'You can play by yourself.'

'How?' He looked genuinely surprised.

'Well . . . you could make up a game. Or look at things, like ships.' She pointed to a huge, rusting cargo boat making its way north towards the Black Sea. It must have discharged its load because it was riding high out of the water.

Hakan wouldn't even look up.

'Anyway,' said Elif giving him another push, 'you could try. My brother Atilla always played games by himself when he was little.'

She remembered Atilla on his own at the edge of the school yard, walking round and round, rather quickly, and singing. Now and again he gave a little hop or a skip, as though he were involved in some complicated routine. If a child asked what he was doing he always replied 'playing' and went on with it even faster than before. He'd made things too: tiny models of people and animals worked from the cellophane and silver paper dropped by other children. His pockets were full of these treasures and he cried when they had got crushed and spoilt.

'Gülfidan Abla says your brother is . . .' Hakan stopped abruptly.

'Is what?'

'Nothing. I've forgotten – ' He wouldn't look at her.

A man selling home-made sweets had stopped outside the park railings. There were golden diamonds of helva, sticky with sugar syrup, and plump little globules of lokum which had been dropped into boiling fat. The toddler pulled briefly and hopelessly at his grandmother's skirt before returning to his excavations. Hakan ran over to the railings at once. Soon he was sitting cheerfully in the middle of the roundabout licking his lips, while Elif ran round and round to keep it turning. After half an hour the park began to fill up with children on their way to school but Hakan hung on to his place, pushing off anyone who threatened to dethrone him. When the school bell began to ring he snatched his rucksack from her hand, rushed off with the others and never even remembered to say goodbye.

A ferry was coming from the opposite shore and was now so close that she realized it was coming in to a landing stage. The decks were crowded with passengers and school children coming over from the European side of the city. Elif could see the white circles of their school collars beneath their upturned faces. As the ferry hooted she made her way curiously along the shore towards where it must land.

The passengers were already disembarking over the rough, shifting boards of the gangplank. They were a slow crowd, shabby on the whole, with the odd, quick movement of the children struggling to push their way to the front to get to school in time. It reminded Elif of the poorer parts of London: the crowds there had always seemed to her similarly grey-faced and quiet. Yet in England things had never been as haphazard as this, surely? She watched as the strengthening breeze fluttered the tattered awning. The vessel shifted. The gap between it and the concrete landing stage widened, showing the blackest of green water. People shouted and the last of the passengers only just stepped off safely. It had made Elif's heart catch in her throat and she cried out. Behind her someone gasped as though they too had been scared. Then they muttered, 'That was a close thing.' Turning round she saw Yaşar. He was as surprised as she was. He stepped aside from his companion whom Elif recognized as the man, Ferhat.

'Are you boarding this ferry too?'

'No. I just came to look.'

'I see.' He smiled. 'Well, maybe you're wiser than me. Did you see how it swung out? It can't have been properly secured.'

'I ate the sweets,' she muttered awkwardly, but he looked mystified and she blushed and realized that he'd already forgotten the gift. Most likely he gave things to all the young girls who visited the stall.

The hooter of the ferry sounded again.

'Have you still got the bag?' he asked.

'What bag?'

'The nâne şekeri bag. That's where you can find me . . . in *that* shop if you . . . wanted . . . anything. Look – I'm sorry, I've got to go.' He ran off and just got across before the sailors drew in the gangplank. At the rail he waved and she waved too and watched the ferry until it was out of sight, just as if it had carried away a real friend.

Back at the house she went through all her pockets and then spoiled the neat piles of clothes in her drawers as she looked for the bag. She hadn't thrown it away because there had been a couple of sweets left. In the end she decided to ask Gülfidan. No one else had been in her room. Elif waited for a quiet moment in the afternoon then she tapped on the door of the guest house. Gülfidan opened it dressed in pyjamas and with her hair dishevelled.

'I'm *so* sorry. Are you ill or something?' Elif was embarassed.

'No I'm *not*. What do you want?' Gülfidan had clearly been asleep.

'It's nothing, it's only about a bag – '

'What bag?' demanded Gülfidan, pushing back hair that was surprisingly thick and shiny. 'I don't know anything about a bag!'

'It's not that sort of bag. It's only a . . . a sweet bag . . . a paper bag . . .' Elif knew that she shouldn't have come. This was the time in the afternoon when lots of people, men and women as well as children, took a siesta. Elif could never get used to it and Zehra Hanım had already complained that she was too noisy. A man's voice called from inside, 'Ask her in, ask her in.' Gülfidan composed herself, flashed a formal smile of welcome and stepped aside.

'No,' protested Elif. The house was small and hot and smelt of unaired rooms. 'I can't stay. It was just – the bag . . .'

'What bag?' asked Ömer eagerly, buttoning up a white shirt. 'Come in, come in, what an honour! Gülfidan, why are you still standing there? Show your visitor where she can sit down. Please, please, don't even think of taking off your shoes. I won't hear of it!' He was fussing like a new housewife, smoothing the divans, hiding things behind cushions and straightening the little crocheted mats that were everywhere.

'What bag is this?' he repeated. Elif, captured like a fly on glue paper, sank deep in a low red chair.

'It wasn't anything,' she muttered. 'The bag wasn't important. I just wanted to . . . to visit you.' Ömer rubbed his hands with pleasure, but his wife recognized the lie and watched Elif's discomfort.

After much whispering they brought her a drink of fruit

juice. It was a thick pinkish brown and slightly sour, as though it had been standing in the sun too long. Ömer stood by the window and watched as she drank, rubbing the plump palms of his hands together.

'I don't suppose she's had anything like that in a foreign country,' he remarked with a foolish grin, as though Elif couldn't hear or couldn't answer or both.

Gülfidan tucked back her thick hair and raised her eyebrows dismissively at her husband.

'I'm sure,' she said, 'that everything is more advanced in England. Much better. Isn't that so, Elif Abla? People only drink cola there, don't they?'

'Cola?' Ömer looked unhappy. 'Why didn't you say? I'd have gone straight out and bought cola. Shall I go now? Would you like cola?'

'No! No, thank you. This is lovely. Very refreshing.' She tipped the glass up to drain it. As soon as it was empty Gülfidan took it from her and returned immediately with a huge pale slab of cheese pie.

'I couldn't,' gasped Elif.

'Why ever not?' asked Ömer. 'It's home-made. It's Gülfidan's speciality. And your brother loves it! Go on. You won't have had anything like it over there. Young Atilla says it's all fast food or frozen. Not that that isn't very good, I'm sure.'

'Maybe she prefers that,' Gülfidan's tone was not friendly. 'It can't be so bad, can it? Not if everybody eats it.'

They watched, as she dug the fork into a corner and began to eat.

'Well?' Ömer's smile was broad and red.

'It's very nice. Wonderfully cooked.'

'There!' He clapped his hands. 'What did I tell you, Gülfidan? I knew she'd like it. And she'll be back for more.

Now eat up. There's more where that came from, and I insist that you treat this home as your home. You're welcome any time of the day or night. Just like Atilla. Now, how about another piece?'

'No, really. I couldn't. I can't finish this . . .'

'Why not?' demanded Gülfidan. Her bold regard had no warmth in it.

'I'm just not used to eating so much. In England – '

'Of course,' said Gülfidan sharply, 'everything's better over there, more scientific.'

'I don't mean that.'

They watched as she swallowed a couple more mouthfuls. The cold oil lay heavily between the layers of thick damp pastry. It dragged on the back of her throat.

A wave of misery engulfed her. Its suddenness, in the middle of this uneventful afternoon, was bewildering. She could have cried. Memories of England were as bright as postcards. Over there it would be the end of the school day. The bell would go, the chairs scrape back over the dusty floors. She could have been slinging her stuff into her bag and looking out for Claire. Emma would shout and run over. They'd buy crisps on the way home and eat them walking down the street. It wasn't anything special at all, but she missed it so much.

She felt the creeping treachery of tears but changed them into a cough, and said that it was a crumb of cheese that had got stuck.

'That'll be the goat's cheese,' explained Ömer. 'It's special. You wouldn't get *that* over there.'

'No,' she nodded numbly.

'I expect you're glad to be here, Elif Abla, glad to have came home, like your brother.'

'Yes.' But she wasn't.

Suddenly she wasn't glad at all and when she finally got away she ran up to her room and flung herself on the bed and cried and cried as though something quite dreadful had happened.

7

Family Life

'Elif?'

'Go away!'

'What's up?' Atilla pushed open the bedroom door and strolled in. 'Have you hurt yourself?'

'No. It's nothing!' How could he still be such a stupid little boy, pretending that people only cried if they shut their fingers in a door or banged their shins? She hadn't cried about things like that for years. And nor had he, to be honest.

He was balancing on the edge of her bed, leaning over, trying to force her face out of the pillow.

'Leave me alone!' she yelled and lashed out sideways with one knee. He didn't let go. Without warning he knelt astride her, captured both her wrists in one hand and pulled her arms back and up. It hurt so much her cry dwindled into nothing. Everything but the desire to be free of the pain slipped from her.

'There!' he crowed triumphantly, like some little kid who's just made it to the top of a steep bank. 'Now tell me! It wasn't "nothing", was it?' He was actually smiling as he sat back on his heels and released her. Elif touched the red marks on her wrists.

'What's going on *now*?' Their elder sister's indignant voice startled them both. She stood in the doorway. Volkan clutched at her long skirt; he sucked on a bunched up bit of it and was as pale as she was.

'Nothing's going on,' murmured Elif.

Sevim sighed heavily.

'This really is too much. And it's a bad example for my sons. Fancy fighting at your age.' Her voice was tight with disapproval.

'We weren't fighting,' protested Elif, pulling her shirt down.

'Aren't you ashamed of yourself?' Sevim continued. 'Because I would be. And Refik Bey wouldn't like it at all. Honestly, Elif, at *your* age – '

Atilla sniggered. Sevim's glance flickered unsurely between them, but settled on Elif.

'It isn't as though I haven't got enough to do', her voice was unexpectedly shrill, 'with two children to look after. Have I got to look after two more?'

'I'm *so* sorry,' Elif scrambled from the bed, stricken with guilt. 'I didn't mean to upset you. It was . . . nothing. And honestly, Sevim, you don't have to look after us. I'm here to look after *you*.' Impetuously she put her arm around her sister's shoulder and would have kissed her but Sevim stepped back. 'Tell me what to do, Sevim, and I'll do it. I want to help.'

'There isn't anything. Nothing at all,' Sevim looked down at her plump white hands where the nails were bitten right away. 'I only want a little bit of peace in my own house, if that's not too much to ask.' Now she raised those hands to either side of her forehead and pressed them there as though she might have had one of her headaches again. Then she sighed and went away with the little boy stumbling silently behind her.

Atilla immediately exploded into loud laughter.

' "And Refik Bey wouldn't like it at all"!' he mocked and, snatching up Elif's night-dress, he folded it over his head in imitation of his elder sister's scarf. Then, stuffing a pillow up his T-shirt he aped her waddling gait.

'Don't, that's beastly.' Elif looked away, embarrassed, although it was funny. 'Poor old Sevim can't help it. Anyway I thought you'd changed your tune about Refik. You usually suck up to him nowadays.'

'So what?' Atilla demanded. He was looking at himself in the mirror and fiddling amongst Elif's make-up things. She wanted to tell him to leave her stuff alone.

'I thought,' Elif began carefully, 'that you liked Refik Abi more than you used to . . . that you . . . liked it here, in his house.'

'I never said that.' Atilla looked up from beneath lashes loaded with mascara. 'All I said was that I didn't want to go back to England.'

'That's not true, Ati. You told me that you *couldn't* go back.'

'Same thing.' He pulled the top from a lipstick.

'No it isn't. And don't – '

'Don't what?'

'Nothing. I just thought you were in danger in England. You know, from those boys. Please don't use that.'

'Why?'

'I haven't got much left.'

'Honestly, Elif! You are such a selfish cow! Have it!' He flung the tube down with such force that it broke.

'I'm *not* selfish!'

'You are! Look at you, getting all worked up over some trashy lipstick, when you can get hundreds of them in the bazaar. And cheaper. And you'd still look ugly with that stupid hair, however much lipstick you wore. But oh, no, you're as bad as Sevim: whine, whine, whine, all day long.'

'I don't whine,' but she heard an unpleasant shrillness in

her voice, 'and I'm not selfish. For heaven's sake, Ati, I stayed in Turkey because of you. I did it for you. You begged me to.'

'I didn't.'

'You did! That time on the beach when you'd been swimming, you begged me. You said that there were people after you. You frightened me, Ati, and you were frightened yourself.'

'I wasn't. You're just making a drama out of it. *You* wanted to stay and I gave you an excuse. Anyway, I'm not begging now.'

'What do you mean?'

'Go back, if you like. *I* don't care. I don't want you here. I've got new friends, people who'll take care of me.'

'But, you said you needed me.'

'That was true *then*. But it isn't now. So go, if you want.'

'I can't. Not now.'

'Why not?'

'Well, Sevim needs me. And term's already started.' She knew that these excuses were feeble.

At that moment Zehra Hanım's voice rang through the house, demanding that Gülfidan come at once. They heard steps running to answer.

'Seems to me that Sevim's got more than enough help.' Atilla grinned and she detested him for being right. 'So, you and I might as well settle in and enjoy ourselves. If you're not going back to England, that is . . .'

He pulled out one of her drawers, and began to poke around.

'Don't!'

'Oh! Why not?' He was smiling, winningly.

'Because – '

'There!' he screamed suddenly. 'Listen to yourself:

"don't, don't, don't". And why not? Because *you* say "no". Wow! Am I scared! What are you going to do then? Slap me? Go on. Try.'

She took a step towards him. Quick as a flash he pulled the whole drawer out, glanced at her, then, in what seemed a moment of madness, he let it go so that everything fell out and smashed and spilt over the floor. Then he skipped from the room spluttering with laughter.

'You naughty girl!' Hakan, just home from school and attracted by the crash overhead, had run straight upstairs without taking off his shoes. Now he knelt beside Elif and surveyed the rubble of underclothes and spilt powder and scattered jewellery.

'It was an accident,' she said, and put a hand out towards him. He snuggled close and stroked her hair, as though he understood. Then he picked out a bra now covered in biscuit crumbs and eye-shadow, and dangled it from one finger, giggling helplessly. Elif sniffed and wiped her eyes.

'Get the dustpan, there's a good boy.'

'All right!'

He ran off, delighted to help, but turned in mid-flight and charged back.

'Don't worry, Elif Abla, I won't *tell*,' he gasped.

'It doesn't matter if you do.'

'But I won't. I promise.'

'All right.' She wanted to question him but didn't. Then she saw the paper bag tightly folded in a corner. It was damp with spilt scent and covered in strands of hair. 'Ferhat Güney ve Kardeşler', 'Ferhat Güney and Brothers', was printed over a motif of nuts and fruits heaped on scales; beneath was the address of the shop. It was in one of the villages further along this shore of the Bosphorus.

'I didn't tell,' Hakan repeated conspiratorially as he watched her sweep up.

'Why not?'

'She'd have been cross with you.'

'Who'd have been cross?'

He didn't reply, only dipped his finger into the powder and sniffed it. Then he jumped up and ran off, his shoes pounding down the stairs.

But it had been an accident, hadn't it? A typical boy's accident. After all, people like her mother always grumbled about how clumsy men were, especially youths of Atilla's age. People said that they couldn't help themselves. Perhaps the drawer had been heavier than he'd expected. Nevertheless the incident proved how hopelessly immature Atilla was. She couldn't possibly leave him on his own, not yet.

Then she saw him in the garden. He was coming out of the Akbuluts' house, but not with either Ömer or Gülfidan. His companion was a tall young man whom Elif recognized as Yusuf, Gülfidan's brother. They kissed and shook hands before Yusuf returned to the house. Elif saw a hand in the guest house drop a lace curtain which had been held aside. Atilla ran jauntily into the street.

That evening Elif dialled home to England.

'Hello? Elif? Is that you, dear?' Her mother sounded surprised. In the background the theme tune to *EastEnders* was playing loudly. 'Is Atilla all right, Elif?'

'Yes, he's fine. And you?'

'Busy, of course. But business is good, so we mustn't complain. And you, dear?'

'Me? I'm fine too, Mum.'

'And Atilla?'

'Actually, he's out, at the moment.'

'That's nice. And what about my darling grandsons?

77

Couldn't you put that rascal Hakan on, just for a minute?'

When Hakan had finished telling his grandmother about his day in school he put the phone down. She had sent her love to everyone, he said, and she wanted him to write a real letter to her, all on his own. He began to rush about, demanding proper writing paper and then an envelope and a stamp too. Volkan, who could not even write his name, began to cry because he wanted the same.

Refik Bey looked up from reading the newspaper.

'Ask your Elif Abla,' he suggested. They fell on her like puppies, tumbling and scratching in their eagerness to be first. As she led them from the room, Refik Bey shook out the pages and began to read a new article. Sevim picked something from her skirt then folded her hands carefully so that the bitten nails were hidden away. She rested her head on the back of her chair.

Elif settled the boys at a table. When they were quiet she imagined her parents sitting in front of the television. If she had been there she would have been finishing her homework upstairs; she had disapproved of all their TV watching, had never understood how they could leave it on, hour after hour, chattering and glittering in the corner like some impossibly demanding relative. Sometimes she'd banged on the floor because of the noise, but they hadn't taken much notice. Still, it had been nice up in her room, with her parents just downstairs. Outside, in the unending neon sunset of a suburban night, the tail-lights of cars had flowed along the black roads like lava which would never cool. She used to glance at her watch: ten minutes more French, then she would phone Claire or Emma. Often they phoned her, and if it was Friday, or nearly Friday, they would make plans for the weekend: arrange to meet up and try things on and recycle a bit more gossip.

On Saturdays her father dragged her along to do the weekly shop. Every week, without fail, he chose the busiest time in the afternoon when things were being snatched off the shelves and rebellious children squatted in front of plastic toys and wouldn't move. Granulated sugar crunched underfoot and the fruit that was left was dimpled with thumbprints. She got her revenge by insisting on reading the information on packets of things that all tasted more or less the same, so that her father was stranded with the trolley, in everybody's way. He never complained and didn't mind when she popped in odd things for herself: more tights, new mascara and little bottles of nail varnish. Back home, she'd try the things out: paint her toe-nails black and imagine that Frankie was lounging by the window, watching her. Sometimes, when her friends came round, Atilla would turn his music up so loud that the whole house shook. She would tell him off but he never remembered. He never had friends round. In fact he never did anything at all, so sometimes she took pity on him and let him go with her to the cinema or window shopping, or just for a walk. Then the girls charged around arm in arm, laughing at anybody and anything. Claire had always said that Atilla was such a darling that she could have taken him home: her own brother was a pig.

Atilla had depended on Elif for everything. She even used to go to his parents' evenings at school and everybody had agreed how responsible she was. She was hurt that he didn't want her help now. Still, when he started school again, that would change. His Turkish had never been that good and he'd want all the help he could get. Once he'd got piles of homework he'd need her. She imagined them sitting together at this table, while she corrected his grammar and quickly worked through his French.

She turned back to her young nephews who were quarrelling over the last piece of writing paper. They'd spoilt the rest of the pad and torn out the scribbled sheets.

'What shall I say?' Hakan demanded. 'Tell me what to say, Elif Abla.'

'And me! Tell me!' Volkan echoed, trying to force his pencil into her hand.

'Say, "Dear Grandma, it was lovely to speak to you." ' Hakan pulled a face, already losing interest. 'Look – shall *I* write the letter?' she suggested. 'I could write one letter for all of us. You could sign your names at the bottom.'

'OK. But tell her about me first,' shouted Hakan, 'everything about me.'

'And me first, too . . .' yelled Volkan.

She retrieved some of the sheets, smoothed them out, and began to write:

'Dear Mum,

Atilla and I have both settled very happily here in Istanbul . . .' The children had run off.

Then she began to cry. Tears dropped onto the paper so that the ink ran. Upstairs she could hear the beginnings of the bedtime war between Sevim and her sons. It was the same every night. At least Ati had never been like that.

But she couldn't stop crying.

When he'd been little, and their parents were working at night to build up the business, he'd often crept into her bed. She'd woken in the early morning with her shoulders and back cold and his soft fair hair tickling her neck.

She wiped her sleeve over her face and looked at her watch. It was late. Those kids should have been in bed hours ago. And Atilla should have been home. In England, he would have been safely in the room next door lying on his bed, listening to his music, his eyes closed and the fingers of one hand tapping the beat. He wouldn't have been somewhere out there, in this huge city, which he didn't know.

Misery, which she had never even suspected, clenched her shoulders up. She imagined him loitering in unlit streets, staring into the dark, cold waters of the Bosphorus. It was unbearable. If she held her breath and tightened her neck a little more, she felt as though her head would have just floated away, with her eyes still weeping sticky, salty tears.

'Elif! Elif?' her sister's voice was loud. 'I've said you'll tell them a bedtime story. I promised. I hope you don't mind.'

They passed in the doorway and if Sevim saw the shine of tears on her sister's face she didn't say a word. Upstairs the boys called eagerly:

'Sit on *my* bed, Elif Abla!'

'No! Don't sit on *his*! Sit on *mine*! Please!'

She perched midway on the chest of drawers. Down in the guest house a yellow light shone behind lace curtains. She turned back to the children.

'Once there was, and once there wasn't, and always in the very middle of it – '

'I don't want one of those stupid *old* stories,' grumbled Hakan, who recognized the beginning of a fairy tale.

'How do you know it's going to be "stupid"? All sorts of stories can begin like that.'

'They can't, Elif Abla. Proper stories begin – "And suddenly – " '

'All right. And suddenly – '

Then they heard the noise. Someone had cried out. Instantly the little boys snuggled down beneath their covers as though caught unawares by irresistible sleep. Volkan, whose eyes were very tightly shut, began to stuff the corner

81

of his quilt into his mouth. Then they heard it again: a scream cut off.

'I expect', said Hakan, 'that it's cats.' His eyes never left Elif's face.

'I'm not sure,' she began.

'I am,' he said energetically. 'It *is* cats. Mummy says it's always cats, just nasty cats out fighting in the night.'

'I think I'd better have a look.'

'No!' they shouted together, but she left the room.

She had remembered one afternoon in England when she got home from school late. The front door had been left open. She'd noticed it from the gate and run up the concrete path.

'Hello?' she'd called. 'Hello? Is anyone home?' Atilla's jacket and bag weren't on the hall chair. Then she thought she'd heard this sound, this smothered cry. When she went into the kitchen, Atilla had been quite alone. He had been slumped at the kitchen table, his jacket still on, his rucksack still slung from one shoulder.

'I . . .' he began.

'What? You what?'

'I . . . I don't . . . feel well,' he'd whimpered, his face buried in his arms. She had tried to find out what the matter was but he'd rushed upstairs and locked himself into the bathroom.

She'd forgotten all about it until now. She hadn't told her parents; she hadn't wanted to worry them and he'd been fine in the morning. She hadn't given it another thought until now, when this cry drew her back as inevitably as the line draws in the hooked fish. Running downstairs she wondered, briefly, if people ever died of fear.

There was no need. Atilla wasn't even in the living-room. It was undisturbed. Sevim was adjusting her scarf, smoothing it down neatly around her pale face. Refik Abi was standing near her. The newspaper lay on the floor between them, its pages disarranged as though it had been flung down.

'I thought I heard . . . Atilla,' whispered Elif.

'No,' Refik Bey's voice was a little louder than usual. 'I think he's still at the Akbuluts'.'

'The Akbuluts? But I saw him go out . . .' To hide her confusion Elif picked up the paper and began to straighten it out. There, caught between its pages was a little tangle of dark hair. She flicked it off and would have folded the pages neatly if Refik Bey had not taken them from her.

'Filth,' he said. 'They print nothing but lies and filth!' The room was very quiet. Elif said goodnight to no one in particular and tiptoed upstairs.

She didn't switch on the light but placed a chair by her window so that she could see the guest house. Then she settled down to watch. When she woke later, moonlight was streaming in but the light behind the lace curtains was out. She stood up, stiff and cold and rubbed at the ache in her neck.

Why should she worry if Atilla hadn't come back? If he preferred to spend his evenings with the Akbuluts, let him! She didn't undress but pulled the covers over her head and drew her knees up to her chin. Then, the only thing that she was aware of was the quick, warm beating of her own heart.

8

A Season of Gifts

A couple of evenings later Refik Bey came home with presents. There was something for everyone but Sevim's, he hinted, was extra special. He held it back to last. Hakan and Volkan were already zooming their new battery cars into the legs of the coffee table and Zehra Hanım had broken into a box of marzipan sweets. Atilla and Elif each received a pair of slippers: Refik Bey had obviously noticed that they didn't have their own to wear indoors and so took the ones intended for guests. Elif slipped her foot into one of hers: it was made of pink leather and almost elegant, in an old-fashioned way, with its high heels and a pattern worked in silver over the toes. She heard her sister gasp. Refik Bey was holding a small package just out of his wife's grasp. They had all been intrigued by the rustle of paper as he drew it from his jacket pocket. A slight flush softened Sevim's face and she was smiling as though she might have guessed what lay within the tissue.

'For the mother of my lovely sons,' said Refik Bey, finally letting the gift drop into her hand. She held it in her palm for a few seconds as though guessing its weight. Her colour deepened.

'Hurry up,' urged Atilla.

She unwrapped a gold bangle which was heavier and more elaborate than the ones she usually wore.

'Wow!' Atilla leant over excitedly and ran his finger around the boldly worked twists of the pattern; as he did so he knocked something else from the paper. It rolled towards Elif but he snatched it up like a beggar taking a dropped coin from the pavement; only it wasn't a coin. It was a tiny gold bangle.

'For my daughter,' explained Refik Bey. 'This is for my daughter, my lovely baby girl.'

'It's bad luck', said Zehra Hanım sharply, 'buying gifts for a baby before it's born.'

'Rubbish, Mother!' he rubbed his hands irritably around his beard. 'That's just superstition. I *know* this new baby will be a daughter. Won't it, Sevim? And if not this baby, then certainly the next!'

'Well . . .' Sevim already had the bangle on her wrist. It was magnificent, and must have been very expensive. She turned her arm this way and that, so that they could all admire it. Then she smiled at Refik with an expression that Elif had never seen before.

'You are *so* good to us, Refik Bey,' Gülfidan whispered from the corner of the room where she was stacking the dirty dishes. 'So generous. So thoughtful.' She was staring at Elif's foot in the pink heeled slipper. 'And fancy him knowing your size so perfectly, Elif Abla, isn't that something? Aren't you lucky to have someone looking after you like that?'

Refik Bey cleared his throat as Gülfidan left the room.

'Didn't you get anything for her?' hissed Zehra Hanım.

'No. No, I didn't. I've done a lot for the Akbuluts recently. What with Yusuf and everything.'

'Yusuf?' asked Atilla unexpectedly. 'You mean Gülfidan Abla's brother?'

'That's right,' said Zehra Hanım importantly. 'My son, God bless him, paid for all Yusuf's education, because Yusuf was such a clever little boy. And *so* pious. Refik is a great benefactor. To deserving cases.'

'Come, come, Mother, you're embarrassing me. It's no more than my duty – our duty – to help the less fortunate. Isn't that right, Sevim?' He had taken hold of his wife's wrist and was inspecting the bangle himself. 'It is a lovely thing, even if I say so myself. The moment I saw it I knew I had to have it. The goldsmith is a good friend.'

Under cover of the table Elif had slipped her foot back into her own trodden-down shoe.

'I think it's terrific!' said Atilla.

'So you like it, do you?' Refik Bey held Sevim's arm towards Atilla.

'It's great. You don't see stuff like that in England. And I bet it cost a bomb. A real bomb – '

'Ati, shut up!' Elif was dreadfully embarrassed but Refik Bey laughed.

'It certainly did,' he said, 'but she's worth it.' He smiled down at his wife before releasing her arm.

'Have you ever thought about that business, Atilla? A bright young fellow like you who appreciates nice things could do very well in the gold market. Very well indeed. And you speak English. It could be useful. I do have connections, there, if you are interested.'

'But he's going back to school,' interrupted Elif.

'Pardon?' Refik Bey turned towards her. The room fell silent as he repeated his question.

'What did you say?'

'I said, "He's going back to school". Atilla has to go to school, he's not fourteen and he should be in school now.' Nobody spoke. Nobody even moved.

'Should he?' asked Refik Bey.

'Well – yes, he should. Really. That's what Mum and Dad said. It's what they expected. Not him working. Not yet . . .' She couldn't stop herself. It was as though everyone else could hold their breath while she was condemned to speak out. Even the little boys crouched under the table, as still as statues.

'He mustn't work,' she insisted, but her voice wasn't steady.

'Why mustn't I work?' challenged Atilla. Refik Bey raised his eyebrows quizzically and shrugged his huge shoulders. Then he spread his hands wide apart.

'Ask her,' he grinned innocently. 'Ask Elif. *She* seems to know more about your life than you do.'

'I don't,' Elif protested. 'It's just – '

'See? She doesn't, Refik Bey. She doesn't know anything. She just wants to boss me around because she's older. She's always been like that.' He was turning the baby's bangle round and round. 'And she isn't that much older than me.' He stamped his foot.

For once Elif was glad that he was behaving so childishly: at least Refik Bey could see it.

'Would you *like* to work, Atilla?' Refik Bey turned his back on Elif. 'Would you like a job in the gold market, with plenty of money in your pocket? I could ask my friends: see if there's an opening for a bright lad like you. Shall I do that, Atilla?'

'Wow! Yes please, that'd be terrific.'

'But you can't,' Elif cried. 'This is a stupid idea. He can't work, Refik Bey, you don't understand. We can't decide anything. I'll have to phone Mum and Dad. Maybe we should go home to England after all – '

Refik Bey moved fast for a large man. He came round the table and stood so close that she could see the veins in his blood-shot eyes.

'Don't, Elif,' he said coldly, 'don't ever call me stupid again.'

'I didn't mean it like that. I meant – '

'I don't care what you meant. I'm telling you now. Don't *ever* call me stupid!' He was shaking with anger.

'Or tell me to shut up!' added Atilla excitedly.

'Why, Elif,' only Sevim's voice was calm, 'you're not wearing your new slippers. Don't you like them? Is it the colour?'

'The colour is fine. And I do like them. They're very nice. Thank you.' She choked on the words.

'Let's see them then.' Zehra Hanım popped another marzipan into her mouth and chewed.

There was no escape. In front of them all she stepped from her trainers into the slippers and took a few awkward steps.

'Very nice,' said Gülfidan, coming back from the kitchen, and wiping her hands on her long skirt. 'So tasteful.' She stared purposefully at Elif's cropped hair. 'You've chosen so well, Refik Bey. Hasn't he, Elif Abla?'

And what could she have said? As she left the room the little boys resumed their car games and Refik Bey asked where the newspaper was. Atilla offered to look for it and pushed past Elif in the hallway.

She drank straight from the kitchen tap, cupping the water in her hand and splashing some over her burning face; Gülfidan returned with the old trainers in her hand.

'They'll do nicely for Melek,' she said straightening the backs.

'What do you mean?' Elif was aware of anger overwhelming misery.

'My young sister Melek, who's still at home. She'll be so pleased with these. She's always very grateful that you're all so good to us. And she's such a humble girl, she'd never expect pink slippers. After all, they'd only get spoilt,

88

wouldn't they, in the shanty town? These'll be fine. She'll love these.'

'But, they're mine, Gülfidan – *I* need them.'

'Oh, dear. Oh, how humiliating. I am *so* sorry. I thought you'd wear your new slippers now. I've made another mistake. But, that's how we do things here, not being educated: we give to those less fortunate, like your brother-in-law said.' She smiled. 'I am *so* sorry. You can see how ignorant I am, not understanding that foreigners do things differently – '

'I'm *not* a foreigner, Gülfidan.'

'No, of course not. If you say so. So here you are: keep your old things. My Melek will just have to make do. As usual.' She sniffed vigorously and muttered that she must have one of 'her heads' coming on.

'But if there's anything you want, Elif Abla, you only have to mention it. You know that I'd crawl from my sick bed to help you.'

She folded her arms and stared at Elif with undisguised scorn.

'You don't have to do that, Gülfidan. All you have to do is leave me alone. And my brother! I don't understand why you hate me, but leave me alone, Gülfidan. Stay away from both of us.'

Elif had never spoken to anyone like that before. She was as shocked as Gülfidan and in the breathless silence which followed her outburst, she snatched back the trainers and stepping out of the slippers left them sprawled untidily in the middle of the kitchen floor, like two dropped pink cakes.

Two days later Atilla began work. Elif had phoned England but her parents had been unconcerned. Maybe, her mother said, it was a job with real prospects. And after all, he'd never done well in England, had he? Maybe he'd make something of himself back home in Turkey.

'And you're fine too?' her mother's voice was full of hope.

'Yes, I'm fine. . . . but life's a bit, well, boring.'

'Well, that's life all over.'

'I suppose so. Has Emma been round?'

'Yes. And Claire. But I told them what a wonderful time you were having with your sister in Istanbul. They were quite envious of you, I could tell at once. These English girls don't have close families like us, do they? Poor things.'

Poor things!

Elif remembered when they had all been younger and she had listened to other girls speculating about being orphans who'd been secretly adopted as babies. How else could they account for these strange and difficult people who were their families and didn't understand them at all? Elif hadn't joined in. She'd thought it rather silly. Now she understood what these girls had meant. Putting the phone down she thought about returning to England. If it wasn't for Atilla she would have left and never come back. But there was no escape. Even if he didn't care about her, she cared about him and always would no matter what he did.

Now, when he set off for work with Refik Bey, she wanted to rush out and drag him back, but it was too late. All she could do was watch.

It was also her fault. If she'd never talked about staying on during that wretched morning on the beach, this would not have happened. Autumn would have come and they would have been safely back in their home in England. They would have been going to school as usual – or she would. But what about Atilla? She had tried to ask him about the gang of boys who had been threatening him, but

90

he would not talk. Once he had hung his head and mumbled something about boys holding a knife to his throat. On another occasion he'd told her that they were forcing him to shoplift for them but when she thought about it she remembered that the shoplifting occurred a couple of years before. Was he lying or had she been unaware of what was happening? Once he insisted that a master had it in for him because he was a Turk. This teacher had knocked him about in the library, then threatened to get him excluded if he reported the incident. When Elif had asked the name of the teacher Atilla had said it was Mr Peaver. 'But wasn't he in primary school?' she had asked in surprise. 'That was his brother, you idiot,' Atilla snapped, 'And they were both pigs, real stinking pigs.' She hadn't known what to say then.

Sometimes she thought that her biggest mistake was in coming to Istanbul. They should have stayed in the South. Down there it would still have been summer, or autumn at the very worst. Here in Istanbul, cold winter winds were already stirring the waters of the Bosphorus and tearing the leaves from the few trees. In the South she and Atilla could have gone to the local secondary school. They would have made friends, because that was how it happened. Sitting side by side in class and catching the same bus every morning, you had to speak to somebody in the end. Why had she been so desperate to stay? Sometimes she was afraid that she hadn't done it for the sake of her sister and the coming baby. She'd done it for herself, because she was scared of something happening to Atilla, something dreadful, which she did not want to face.

Each morning she watched them from her bedroom window: Refik Bey was heavy and dark in his business suit with his collarless shirt buttoned up high and tight at his throat. Atilla followed in new black shoes polished by

Gülfidan who also pressed neat creases into his new trousers each morning. He carried Refik Bey's briefcase and darted forward to open the gate. Ömer would be waiting in the blue Mercedes with the engine running, so that they could shoot off the moment Refik Bey had settled himself into the passenger seat. Years ago Elif and Atilla had giggled as the car sank under the weight, now Atilla's face was straight.

Sometimes she told herself that she was worrying over nothing. What harm could possibly come to Atilla? Nobody could be more careful and correct than their brother-in-law, and this, after all, was the Turkish way, wasn't it? People started young in business. They learnt on the job; that was what her parents had always answered when Atilla complained about helping in the workshop in England. 'You can't start too young,' had been their reply. So was she just being prejudiced? Painfully, she wondered if Gülfidan was right: had she become more foreigner than Turk? Yet she didn't understand what Atilla would actually do. Refik Bey had placed him with a friend, an İbrahim Bey who owned a shop dealing in gold and silver and jewellery in the covered bazaar. So far Atilla had only been allowed to fetch tea and coffee for İbrahim Bey and his friends and customers, but he was enjoying the work, he said. At the end of the first week he came home with his wages.

'How much did they give you?' Elif was unable to contain her curiosity.

'Lots!' he said casually but he was smiling so broadly that she knew he was satisfied.

In fact, everyone in the house seemed to be satisfied, except her. For the first time in her life, no one needed her opinion or cared about it. Even Hakan had grown tired of his English lessons. As the weather got colder he was less keen to walk to school early. Often, he went on his own, at the last minute. Elif missed those outings.

'You should go out more,' advised Zehra Hanım, as Elif sat with her and Gülfidan during one of the endless afternoons. Sevim was upstairs resting: Volkan would be with her, snuggled close.

'Go out!' Elif was exasperated. 'Where can I go?'

'Come to us,' suggested Gülfidan, 'you can always visit us again.'

'There!' cried Zehra Hanım.

'Though of course', Gülfidan bent over the rice again, 'I know you don't want to come and see us. Not truly.'

'Whatever do you mean? Of course she wants to see you. Explain yourself.'

'Oh, Zehra Hanım, it's not my place to explain,' Gülfidan sighed. 'I couldn't possibly. But the invitation is always there. I told Elif Abla the day she arrived: "Our home is *your* home", I said, but she didn't come again. So we have to make do with Atilla Abi, not that he isn't very welcome. He'll be with us tonight. He can't do without my cheese pie. I don't know what it is, because I'm only a humble cook. Maybe he only visits because we're humble people and he doesn't want to hurt our feelings . . . '

Gülfidan stood up. The tray of rice that she had cleaned was balanced against her hip. She stopped beside Elif, challenging her to protest.

'I know you told me to leave your brother alone,' she sighed, 'but he just keeps on coming!'

'Well!' Zehra Hanım looked from one to the other of them. She folded her legs under her and settled back against the cushions on the divan: she could have enjoyed a good quarrel before tea. Elif wouldn't oblige. Without saying a word, or glancing at either of them, she left. In the dark hallway she stepped into her trodden-down trainers, took her fleece from the coat stand and pushed open the front door.

Later, as she sat on a bench in the park, she thought about her sister. Sevim wouldn't have answered back, but she wouldn't have run out of the house either. She'd have . . . done nothing, wouldn't she?

She found herself thinking about her sister's marriage. What had it really been like? Elif could remember the ceremony, just about. It had been such a hectic time; a hairdresser had come to the house and Sevim had been transformed. She had changed from an ordinary older sister into this rouged, red-lipped face in the middle of a vast puff of white lacy stuff. Elif and Atilla had watched most of the fun from under a table. The house had been full of people, who weren't interested in them, so being under the table had been a good idea, until Atilla threw up. And Refik Bey . . . What of him? Elif hadn't realized that there was going to be a marriage until suddenly, at the end of the summer holiday in Refik Bey's seaside house, everyone began talking about 'the bride'. She hadn't understood that Sevim was going to be the bride and had said that it wasn't fair. People had laughed and said she'd have to wait. This was Sevim's turn: she was the lucky girl. Sevim had been sixteen, only a few months older than Elif was now. Whatever had she thought when she found herself in this house, with Zehra Hanım and Gülfidan, and with her parents and younger sister and brother already far away in England?

Had Sevim ever run from that house and come down here to where dark water lapped against the concrete shore?

9

The Concrete Coast

An hour's walk along the Bosphorus took Elif to a district that she didn't know. In some parts she could stay close to the water but in others, buildings came down to the shore so she had to retreat to the main coast road. It was colder than she had expected with a damp wind blowing in from the European coast on the other side. She maintained a steady pace and swung her arms to keep warm. She wished she'd had a hat or a scarf: though her hair had grown, her ears were freezing.

Men and boys were fishing wherever they could and the catch swam or floated in washing-up bowls and buckets and even cut-off plastic bottles. Little boys ran up and down trying to sell bait or fishing-line and packets of matches or chewing gum. One, with the cracked lips and weather-stained face of a child who has been out on the streets all his life, trotted after her. He was selling gofre, the papery wheels of sweet waffle with a smear of vanilla cream in between. She felt in her pocket for change but didn't have enough.

'Are you a German?' he asked, in his hoarse, old man's voice. When she shook her head and said that she was a Turk he lost interest and ran back to the men along the shore. Another bulk carrier passed down the middle of the waterway on its voyage from the Black Sea. It was heavily laden and low in the water and the wash churning in its wake rippled against the concrete coast and made the fishermen's floats dance wildly.

She was aware of people watching her progress, maybe asking themselves 'and what sort of a foreigner is *that* one?' No one, however, spoke. The silent men, squatting patiently behind their fishing rods, scrutinized her briefly from under the peaks of their caps, then went back to watching the floats. Maybe she attracted attention because nobody else was out walking. She had occasionally seen joggers in the wealthier parts of Istanbul and then there were the poor, who walked long distances to get to places, but they and everyone else seemed to have a reason to be on the streets. Children and students were travelling to and from school and women were either dressed up to visit friends or were carrying bags or shopping. Even a woman begging along a bus queue seemed to excite less interest than Elif did. Was she walking too fast, or too slowly, or did she just not look right? Surely it wasn't only her hair?

If she'd had money in her pocket, she'd have gone shopping too. Then she could have demonstrated that she belonged here, that she needed bread and white cheese like everyone else. She would have gone into a little grocer's shop and chatted, saying exactly the right thing and drawing no second glance. The man would have put aside his cigarette, wrapped the piece of cheese in greaseproof paper and then newspaper and handed back her change, without even looking at her face. She was adrift: out, yet with no place to go. Should she give up and go back to her sister's house? And how could she? How could she suddenly turn round, in the middle of the pavement, and return along the way she had come, without having been anywhere?

Then she saw the shop. Two old plane trees, as mottled and patched as beggar's trousers, grew on either side of a small square. The shop was one of three and she read the sign: 'Ferhat Güney ve Kardeşler'. On one side there was a shop selling knitting wool and materials. On the other was a coffee house with a couple of green wooden tables and chairs standing outside, although nobody sat there on an afternoon like this. Inside men drank tea and coffee. She could see them dimly through the cigarette smoke and the condensation which ran down the window. When the door opened she heard the tumble and click of dice and counters on the backgammon boards. Then, as she watched, Yaşar stepped out. He was with Ferhat. They talked intently, before embracing and parting. Ferhat crossed the grey stone square. Yaşar looked up and called out, 'Good luck', and must have seen her, surely. Ferhat acknowledged the good wishes with a nod and a wave and Yaşar turned back into the shop. In that moment, the secret handful of hope that she had barely been aware of carrying, fell from her grasp, to be blown away by the wind.

It was like not winning the local art competition, years ago. Secretly, Elif had been so sure that she would win. She was certain that her entry was beautiful and skilful beyond words, and she had worked so hard at it. It was way better than most of the other paintings being entered. Some of those hadn't even looked like what they were meant to be and others were just so messy. She had been passionately hopeful of winning right up until the end, even though nobody else seemed to think she even had a chance. Each night, in the moments before sleep, she had savoured the amazing joy of seeing herself declared the winner, or at least of being in the first three. Maybe it was a bit much to expect to be first, straight off! Her picture hadn't even made it into the exhibition. It was just one of hundreds and hundreds left in untidy heaps at the back of the hall, to be 'claimed by their entrants'. Nobody had been the least bit sorry for her. She alone had known the enormity of her disappointment at this destruction of her hopes.

Now Yaşar hadn't even recognized her. Elif pretended to be having trouble with a shoe-lace, so that she had a reason for turning round. He looked back across the square.

'Hey!' he shouted. 'Excuse me! Wait, won't you wait a moment?' He ran over to her, smiling as broadly as if he had only just seen her.

'What are *you* doing here?'

'Nothing! I didn't come on purpose. I was only walking . . .'

'That's all right.' He was watching her closely.

'I . . . I just . . . went for a walk . . . and found myself here. I mean, I didn't *know* your shop was here.'

'Oh dear! That doesn't say much for our advertising campaign.'

I didn't know you had an advertising campaign.'

'We don't. It was a joke. Look, come in, now you're here. You look . . .' he was still staring at her, 'you look . . . frozen through.'

'It's my hair, isn't it? It's much too short. Everyone thinks I look stupid!'

'Surely not. I like it, Elif. It's brilliant, honestly, but I guess that's why I didn't recognize you at first. I've been watching out for someone with long hair, but come in. At least it's warmer in the shop than out here.' He looked at her again. 'You were wearing a hood when I saw you near the ferry.'

He opened the damper at the bottom of the little stove and dropped several bits of wood in at the top so that flames blazed up. Then he fetched one of the chairs from outside the café and put it near the stove for her.

'Do you like salep?' he asked.

'Yes. But I can't stay. I mean, I shouldn't, should I?'

'Why ever not?'

'Well –' Elif looked down. If he didn't understand she couldn't begin to explain. She recalled the exact curve of Zehra Hanım's eyebrows as the old lady recounted with wide-eyed horror recent gossip about a local girl who had been careless in her choice of friends and now could never hope to find a respectable husband. She pictured Gülfidan nodding in eager, scandalized agreement.

'Come on,' he said, 'this is the end of the twentieth century, not the nineteenth, whatever people like your wretched brother-in-law and his friends are trying to do!'

Yaşar had spoken loudly. Beside her the stove roared. She could feel its sudden heat burning one side of her face and she noticed a smell of scorched paint and dust as the chimney pipe got too hot. He kicked the damper shut.

'I'm sorry. I shouldn't have spoken about your sister's husband like that. If you'd rather go home, of course you must, only, at least let me order that salep for you. The café next door is famous for it – they should be! They buy their salep from us.'

'Thank you. That would be nice.'

While he was out she looked around curiously. It was a small shop. A dark wooden counter with a till and scales stood at the back. In front were sacks of grains and seeds and dried herbs, both barks and flowers. Behind the counter large glass jars contained the more exotic wares like pine nuts and resin and sticks of cinnamon. There were skeins of rope and spades and large, hand-made sieves and then, past the boxes of candles and the wicks for the paraffin lamps, there were polythene bags of the brightly coloured pigments which poor people mixed with lime wash when they were repainting their houses. Elif had always thought blue was the prettiest of all. When she was younger and had listened to her parents talking about the house they planned to buy when they finally returned from England, she had always imagined that it would be a little, low village house with a red tiled roof and a garden of flowering fruit trees. Its walls would definitely have been painted this wonderful, gentle blue. When she grew up and was more sensible, she understood that her parents intended to buy a centrally-heated flat in a convenient part of town and that the walls would be concrete and never painted at all. People like them, who had lived and worked in Europe, never settled back into the countryside again.

As the shop warmed up the sweet scents of walnut and vanilla mingled with the peppery smells of cumin and chilli and cloves. The air stirred. Bunches of dried sage and camomile flowers and bundles of roots and leaves which she did not even recognize, spun and swung from nails in the ceiling. They brushed against each other with a sound as soft as indrawn breath.

Yaşar returned with two cups of salep and warned her not to drink hers straight away. The milk, he said, was scalding hot.

'I haven't had this for years.' She closed her hands around the thick, white china, and breathed in the ginger and nutmeg which had been sprinkled on top. 'I suppose that's because it's a winter drink, and we always come back in summer.'

'Do you know what it's made from?'

'Not really. Mum said that it was a sort of cornflour with the spices sprinkled on top. We had a little tin of it years ago in England, but after it was finished we never brought back any more.'

'Actually, it isn't cornflour, not if it's the real thing.' He pointed to a grainy cream powder in one of the glass jars. 'Salep is ground from the dried root of wild orchids. We buy ours from an old man in one of the villages in the Tauros mountains, but it's getting harder and harder to find. I used to miss it when I was in Germany, especially on cold, winter days.'

'I didn't know you'd been in Germany.'

'Surely you've heard my accent?'

'I can hear something. I noticed it when you were at Ahmet Efendi's, but I didn't know that was what it was. Oh well, I suppose you can hear my English one – though everyone says I'm losing it fast. They say that soon I'll sound like a "real" Turk.'

'And you'd like that?'

'Of course. But actually I always thought I did, until I came to Istanbul.'

They must have chatted for over an hour. A couple of customers came into the shop, one for dried mint and the other for corn for his chickens. Apart from that, no one disturbed them and Elif realized that she had been talking as easily to Yaşar as she had ever talked to friends like Claire and Emma.

They could, she thought, have talked for ever, about everything under the sun. She told him about Atilla and how she worried about him. He explained that Ferhat was his elder brother and that they were very close. As evening fell she was unwilling to go. She could have helped him lift the iron shutters into place and locked the door from the inside; they would have drawn down the old, faded blinds. Then she would have put more wood in the stove and inhaled the warm, exciting scents of all those things that she could not yet name. If this wasn't the little blue house on the hillside, it nevertheless felt more like home than anywhere had felt for a very long time. While she sat there, the ugly indifference of a world that did not care for her was kept back. It was as if the warmth of summer had returned.

'It's late,' he said at last, but she stayed where she was, holding her hands out to the stove. She was imagining the little square in an Istanbul spring. The plane trees would have burst into bright green leaf and the sunshine would be flickering through onto his hands as he sat at a table and drank tea. She imagined him talking to friends, to his brother, Ferhat, and they would be talking about –

'Why did you call my brother-in-law "wretched"?' she asked suddenly.

'I'm sorry. I shouldn't have said that.'

'But you did. So why? And that stuff about the nineteenth century: what did you mean?'

'Don't you know?'

'Know what?'

'Don't you know about Refik Bey?'

'Know *what*?' Suddenly, it felt too late and too dark in the little shop. She was afraid of knowing too much, yet could not leave.

'Ahmet Efendi said that you didn't know, that you had no idea. He said he wanted to tell you, but he didn't know how. Elif, why did you stay?'

'I stayed . . . because I wanted to.' She knew that she must sound very stupid. 'I didn't want the summer to end, ever. I never do. But I didn't plan it. It just sort of happened. When Atilla told me about his problems in England and said that he was afraid to return, it seemed the right thing for me to do. And of course there was Sevim. When we were at the seaside, she asked me to help her and I wanted to.'

'And you always wanted to help everyone, didn't you? Even when you were a little girl?'

'How do you know that?'

'Don't you remember me at all, Elif?'

'No. How should I? Anyway, you said you were in Germany for years.'

'But not in the summer holidays. They always sent me back to the village and one summer I stayed with Ahmet Efendi and Hatice Teyze. Don't you remember that summer and the boat trip to Taşlı Ada, Elif, when your sister . . . had the accident?'

She did remember now. She remembered the heat of the sun and the tilt of the shining sea as she jumped in from the side of the boat. And she remembered him, hanging on the oar, holding the boat steady as she leapt.

'That boy was *you*?' she cried.

Ahmet Efendi and Hatice Teyze usually had a grandchild living with them over the summer. That year, the year of the accident, the child had been a skinny, sunburnt lad who could swim like a fish. He had also been very silent: 'insolent' was what Refik Bey had called him, when he hadn't immediately done as he was asked. He had been older than her and Atilla, yet sometimes, as he swept and watered the garden or polished the cars, Elif had noticed him watching them play, as though he wanted to join in, but he never had because he was older and of course there was always work to be done.

He'd come on that trip to the island, sometimes rowing, sometimes squatting in the bottom of the boat baiting the lines for the rest of them. When someone had a bite he would extract the hook from the desperate red throat of the fish. She had swum alongside the boat, sometimes racing it, sometimes just drifting on her back, with her hair floating like silk on the surface. Sevim had come on that trip, leaving the babies behind at the house, even though she wasn't supposed to be out in the sun.

After the wonderful picnic, when the rest of them sought to sleep off the effects of over-eating in the shade of tall, black rocks, or watched the endless roll and dip of the sea, Sevim had gone for a walk. She would be fine on her own, she said, winding her long scarf around her head and throat, against the sun.

It was that boy who had heard something. He'd raced off, leaping from rock to rock and then dived in, to bring her from the water. She had only ventured in knee deep, she said, to cool her burning feet. A single, unlucky step had plunged her down out of her depth. Then the whole weight of the devious ocean had turned her dress and scarf to stone so that she was dragged down and could not get up again.

In the evening when they breathlessly informed Refik Bey of what had so nearly happened to his young wife, he had been angry. Sevim, he said, had been warned not to go into the sun; maybe his wife would listen to good advice in the future.

Nobody had ever spoken of the incident again. It had been entirely forgotten. Now, Elif recalled her sister's face as the boy dragged her in. She remembered how the other women had fussed over Sevim, stroking her white cheek and squeezing the water from her sodden clothes and hair and cursing the sea for its treachery.

'That was *you*?' Elif said. She remembered nothing more about that particular holiday, except some lingering sense that the boy had not been around after the incident. Had he gone back to the village?

'That was me,' he replied quietly. 'And that was your

brother-in-law, even then. That's why I called him "wretched". He wouldn't have cared if your sister had drowned.'

'That's not true! He cares about my sister. He loves her. He's always thinking about her, worrying about her. How can you say such a dreadful thing?'

'Because it's true.'

'It isn't. It can't be. He does care: he even gives her these huge presents . . .'

He looked away, as though he was sorry for her and her childish naivety. She remembered her sister's hand waiting for the tissue-wrapped gift, as though it wasn't such a surprise at all, as though she was half expecting it.

'How do you know this?' she whispered.

'Ahmet Efendi and Hatice Teyze told me.'

'Told you *what*?'

'That . . . that . . . he's unkind to her.'

'What do you mean, "unkind"?'

'I don't know any details.'

She knew that he was concealing something. It was horrid and it frightened her but she did not dare ask him what it was.

'But my sister would have told me, wouldn't she? And why did Refik Bey ask me to stay? He wouldn't have wanted me around if he had something to hide, would he?'

Then she remembered how they had been left in the summer house by the sea. Perhaps Refik Bey hadn't wanted them in Istanbul after all.

'I'm sorry,' Yaşar said, 'but I had to say something. I wanted you to know so that you can be on your guard.'

'On my guard? But against *what*?'

'He's a powerful man now, your brother-in-law.'

'Powerful?'

'And he's got influential friends, political friends. They've changed things in Turkey and they want to change them even more. They want to see a return of the şeriat, the religious law, and to undo lots of the reforms which Atatürk brought in. They want to take us back not just to the nineteenth century, but to the Middle Ages and if that ever happened, there would be no place here for people like you and me and our brothers. You, a girl on your own, could never walk down the street again, with those curls blowing in the wind. My brother could never write what he wants; they'd censor all that. Refik Bey won't let people like you and me live our lives as we want.'

'But Refik Bey doesn't take any notice of *me*. He doesn't care about me. It's . . . Ati . . .' she could barely speak. 'It's my brother he's interested in. He takes Atilla to work in the morning and Ati's as obedient as a little dog. What have I done, Yaşar? I've delivered my brother into their hands.'

'Maybe it's all a mistake.'

'It isn't though, is it?'

He didn't answer, only went next door to the coffee house and brought back a friend with a taxi who would take her home.

10

When Snow Falls

One morning Gülfidan was leaning over the gate. She had hung out the washing and thrown soapy water down the steps to clean them. She lingered there chatting, apparently, to someone on the road, even though it was bitterly cold. Her feet, in plastic slippers, were bare and red. Now and then she glanced up at the house, but Elif, hidden behind the curtains in her room, took care not to be seen. Out on the street other people hurried about their business, wrapped up against the cold. Children were so bundled into coats and scarves that they appeared to roll rather than walk. Only the poor looked much the same, their faces grey and set as they grit their teeth to stop themselves shivering and rubbed their hands which were puffy with cold. Elif had never thought that Istanbul could be so wintry.

It had snowed for a couple of hours the day before and Hakan and Volkan had rushed out and made a tiny, muddy snowman, about the size of two grapefruits. That snow had melted leaving a sea of mud but it was still bitter. The sky was low and grey and full. It would snow again. The steps which Gülfidan had just swept, steamed faintly and in the cracks and corners a few bubbles sparkled incongruously. And still Gülfidan stood there, as if on guard, and impervious to the cold.

It had been the same all week. Nothing had been said but around the time Hakan set out for school, Gülfidan was always there by the gate. She straightened his clothes and smoothed his hair again and checked that he had the essentials for school: a clean hanky, his lunch-box and a little money too. Sometimes she gave him something from her own pockets but Elif was too far away to see whether it was sweets or money or something else altogether. Gülfidan never accompanied the boy to school but her presence ensured that Elif didn't either.

Nothing much had been said in the house all week. The taxi which brought Elif back had dropped her at the far end of the street and as she approached the house she saw that it was lit up like a department store. Every single light must have been on. She imagined those inside running up and down looking for her and later she was certain that one of them had been in her room again, going through her things, but they hadn't said anything to her, not directly. Zehra Hanım had sniffed and raised her eyebrows when Elif stepped into the house, remarking sarcastically that she hoped she had had a 'nice walk'. Next time she wanted some fresh air, maybe they could go to one of the parks together; then they could have tea and pastries and if Ömer took them by car, they wouldn't have to walk in the street at all. But they would have to wait until spring, naturally.

'Until spring?' echoed Elif, but she managed to smile as though spring might not be years and years away. Gülfidan, leaning against the door with her arms folded across her chest, commented that she'd heard that foreigners thought walking was good for the health, though she herself, with all *her* work, never had the time for it.

Then the doorbell had rung and the four of them who were still standing close together in the hallway, fell silent instantly. Sevim straightened her scarf and stepped forward as usual. Refik Bey didn't carry a key. He knew, he said, that the women would always be home to welcome him.

108

Elif, desperate to see Atilla, darted in front of her sister.

'I'll do it!' she cried, flinging the door open. Her brother wasn't there.

'Where is he?' She pushed past Refik Bey but there was no one behind him on the path.

'Where's Ati?' she demanded. 'What's happened?' There was panic in her voice.

'Atilla?' Refik Bey looked puzzled. 'Oh, he's working late. İbrahim Bey has something on.'

'What do you mean, "something on"?'

'What do you *think* I mean, my dear?' He was smiling indulgently, as though she were a silly little girl. Sevim helped him out of his coat and Gülfidan knelt down to put his slippers ready.

'Is he working in the covered bazaar?' insisted Elif.

'Yes. Why not?' Then he winked. 'My goodness, young lady, give your brother some freedom. You're worse than a mother-in-law!'

He laughed and the other three laughed too; then he shouted for his sons and asked them if they had been good boys and when they said they had he gave them a bar of chocolate each and sent them off to play quietly so that he could read his paper.

It was late when Atilla came in. Elif was roused by the click of the latch and a tread that was too cautious and careful on the stairs.

'Atilla?' she whispered, opening her bedroom door. Someone stopped in the darkness but did not reply.

'Atilla? Is that you?'

He must have gone downstairs again. Was he hiding from her? Had something happened that he did not want her to see? She switched on the light and ran towards him in uncontrollable terror but it wasn't Atilla at all. It was

Gülfidan who faced her from the bottom of the stairs.

'Oh dear! Oh, you must forgive me! Now I've woken you up. How clumsy I am. My dear Elif Abla, I'm *so* sorry!'

'You didn't wake me.'

'No?' A moment of doubt lined the woman's handsome face. She pushed back her huge, bright swathe of newly hennaed hair.

'I was waiting for Atilla.'

'For Atilla?' Gülfidan sounded relieved. 'He was back hours ago. Well, I must get on, if there's nothing else that you want . . .'

'I never wanted anything!'

'No?'

'No!' They had raised their voices. Overhead one of the children whimpered in his sleep.

'Can I go now?' asked Gülfidan. Elif nodded and when the woman hurried away her new pink high-heeled slippers tapped noisily over the kitchen floor.

When Elif looked into her brother's room, Atilla turned over to reveal one flushed cheek, creased with sleep. He swallowed and sighed and his eyelids flickered as if he might wake, but he didn't. He looked at peace. His slim boy's arm was thrown back on the pillow behind his head and the upturned palm of his hand was as soft and pink as it had been when he was a tiny boy, and slept in the bed beside hers. Was she being stupid, and frightening herself over nothing? He looked absolutely fine – better, if anything, than he used to. His clothes were new, his shoes polished, his wages were piling up in a shoe-box under the bed. Who was she to disapprove? And what of Gülfidan? Even if the woman began work at 4 o'clock in the morning, this wasn't Elif's house so why object? What happened in the middle of the night had nothing to do with her, Elif told herself.

Maybe that was the way things were done here, and she was the one out of step. This wasn't her home and her country any longer. She didn't fit in and was in everybody's way. It was like outgrowing a favourite pair of shoes: you might jam your feet back in, but you'd never be comfortable and it would be impossible to walk any distance.

Then she thought about Yaşar. Was she acting like a dumb teenager, believing everything he said, just because she liked him? So what had he said, exactly? After all, lots of people were 'unkind' to each other, whether they were married or not and she hadn't understood what he'd said about politics. Her parents never discussed anything like that at home: politics, they said, was 'a dirty game' and not something that decent, hardworking people like themselves need bother about. And what of Yaşar's obvious dislike of Refik Bey? He had clearly hated him as a boy, but that wasn't enough. If she was honest, she had never liked her brother-in-law either.

Refik Bey had remained the stranger that he always had been – and if her elder sister had become a stranger too, maybe that was what marriage did to women. Maybe they did become someone else when they changed their names. And Sevim, after all, had been so young when she married. She had been a schoolgirl, expecting to start a new school in England, living with her parents. Now she was all grown-up with a life and a home of her own.

And Atilla . . . ? Was he to grow up here, with a life of his own, and become a stranger to her as well? Or had he already become that stranger? For a week Elif had remained in the house, trying to reconcile herself to what was happening.

Down in the garden, Gülfidan had finally moved away from the gate. She picked up the red plastic bowl and the brush and came slowly back up the steps. At the top she paused and stared at the sky as though calculating when more snow would fall and spoil her handiwork. For one moment Elif recognized her beauty, saw the striking woman she could have been if she was not endlessly sweeping the mud from their steps, with her own feet bare and reddened with cold and her face rough and lined. Had she misjudged Gülfidan too? Guiltily she remembered how she had disliked her the moment they met. She was ashamed of it now. She had never given the Akbuluts a chance, whereas Atilla had become their friend. He accepted the hospitality which they offered in their little, close room. He drank their tea and even liked their food. He accepted them the way they were and they, it seemed, liked him. Could it be that for the first time in their lives Atilla was right and she was wrong?

In two minutes she had changed into her warmest clothes, taken a handful of notes from the shoe-box under Atilla's bed and was on her way out. Nobody tried to stop her. She hurried down the street and asked which dolmuş would take her into the centre of Istanbul. There were conflicting replies. When she mentioned that she was going to Kapılı Çarşı, the covered market, a woman with a young child looked up.

'I'm going there,' she said, 'come with me.'

They found two seats at the back of an ancient dolmuş and Elif was glad to be squeezed in there, out of the cold. The child, whose face was almost hidden by a thick pink scarf, reached over suddenly and prodded one of Elif's half-grown curls with a tiny, pink-mittened fist. The mother told it not to, but it did it again and Elif guessed from a glimpse of its sparkling eyes that deep down, beneath all that pink, fluffy wool, it was laughing at her.

'It's all right,' she said. 'I don't mind a bit. I know that my hair looks funny.'

'Oh, no! It's not funny. It's very smart and, I must say, you do speak awfully good Turkish for a foreigner.'

'I'm not a . . .' began Elif, then saw how the other bit her lip in embarrassment. 'Well, yes. I suppose I am a foreigner. I was born here but I've lived most of my life in England. Actually, I'm only here on holiday. I'm going back soon.' The unexpected relief that this lie gave Elif was enormous. It warmed her like the endless touch of the summer sun on her skin.

'I'm going back,' she continued easily, 'but I'm leaving my brother here. He's started work and wants to stay but I've decided to return. That's where I'm going now: to see my brother at work and to tell him about my decision.'

They sat together in companionable silence as the dolmuş jolted and creaked its way through the heavy traffic. In the close atmosphere of smoke and heavy winter clothes the child's eyelids drooped and it began to nuzzle the woolly covering around its thumb. They crawled across one of the suspension bridges over the Bosphorus which linked the Asian and European shores. The woman sighed: it was a dreadful journey, she said and they'd have to change dolmuş on the other side, but she still did it twice a week, and had done ever since she married. She missed her own family so much and could understand how anyone must feel about leaving a young brother behind.

'We're not that close,' Elif shrugged, 'not now.' She was amazed at the ease with which she could continue lying. Her heart did not even beat faster.

They finally reached one of the entrances to Kapılı Çarşı nearly an hour later. The woman, with the sleeping child in her arms, hurried away down the street. Elif approached

113

the group of food stalls and street sellers clustered around the entrance. Balloon sellers, porters with baskets strapped on their backs, and smartly dressed workers from offices jostled each other. In a corner a boy crouched by a small fire, feeding rubbish and smashed boxes into the yellow flames.

Kapılı Çarşı was one of those famous places which she'd always been aware of and thought she knew well, yet wasn't sure if she'd ever actually stepped inside it. Friends in England certainly had: they'd shown her postcards and guidebooks and asked if she knew the gold market or the book market or the special streets where embroidered tablecloths or glass or towels were sold. She'd always answered 'yes', because she could imagine it so vividly, but she was never sure if she was remembering Kapılı Çarşı or the markets in Ankara which she visited as a small child. She could even be confusing them with those of Antalya or Izmir.

If she had been here before she'd never understood how vast Kapılı Çarşı was: it was a whole hidden world with its own streets and customs. Today it was not particularly busy, nor were there many tourists, yet within moments of entering she began to doubt that she would ever find the place where Atilla worked. There must be thousands and thousands of tiny shops and they all looked similar. The window displays of carpets and rugs, of leather jackets and cheap clothes, of brass and copper, all resembled each other. Even the young men who lounged in the doorways and beckoned her in, were similarly dressed and the music drifting from their tape decks was all the same.

Was this what Atilla did? Did he spend his days listening to singers and watching the tourists go by? And if he did, what was wrong with that? She wasn't going to criticize

114

him. She just wanted to know, to observe him in this new life and see if he was happy. That was why she'd come.

She wanted to ask for directions to İbrahim Bey's shop, but she was afraid of being surrounded by dozens of little boys selling key-rings and lighters and foreign cigarettes: she could never approach the shop unobserved with them swarming around. She had already turned away from the outstretched hand of a beggarwoman who sat with a silent, crippled son on newspapers beside a drinking fountain.

In front of her a small group had gathered outside a quilt makers. They must be from a village or one of the shanty towns on the outskirts of the city. The men were thin and dark with leathery, brown necks inside threadbare shirt collars and patched jackets. The women were thick-set and noisy with checked woollen shawls around their heads and shoulders; they wore no coats, only knitted cardigans over a couple of dresses. They had just come out of the shop and were arguing about something. In the window an elderly man glanced up with an amused expression on his face, then resumed stitching the geometric patterns into the plump, crimson satin of the quilt on which he worked. A display of bridal quilts hung at the back of the shop. A young girl stood at the edge of the group, staring at her legs and feet in unaccustomed stockings and ugly high-heeled shoes. This girl, Elif realized, must be the bride. Was she thirteen? Fourteen? This could be a trip to complete her trousseau and one of those women haggling over prices would be the mother, determined that her daughter should not go cheaply. The bridal bed, at least, would be the best she could buy. The girl, who was plump and fair with a child's red cheeks as downy as a peach, scratched herself and rocked from side to side on the shoes. Was one of those men the bridegroom?

Years ago, when Sevim's trousseau had been hurriedly bought, had her sister also watched with such indifference? The girl caught Elif's eye and in that glance took in her slim, boyish outline, her jeans and fleece and trodden-down trainers. She swiftly scrutinized Elif's absurd black curls that were more like ruffled feathers than anything else and then, instead of looking away, she grinned, shyly at first then quite boldly, as though they might have been friends had they known each other; at least they could enjoy this joke of a marriage. Elif smiled back: at the moment when she felt herself most a stranger, everything was reaching towards her saying, 'Stay. You can be one of us.'

Then she heard a noise. Deeper inside the market people were shouting. Both Elif and the girl heard and looked up. The others were still busy with the purchase, but there was a thunder of running feet and a cry of, 'Dur! Yakala!' 'Stop! Arrest him!' It was the cry of a chase. The bridal party heard it now. They moved away from the window and peered up and down the narrow passageway. People came out of the nearby shops.

The man from the quilt shop looked up with the silver thimble still on his finger and a crimson cotton hanging from between his teeth like a thread of blood. The noise rolled nearer. Quickly he threw aside his work and jerked at the iron shutters. He called them to step inside. Somewhere quite near, something was overturned: metal and wood tumbled and hit glass which shattered onto the flagstones in a violent waterfall of sound.

'Hurry!' he shouted.

Someone pounded by, caught a foot on the edge of the drinking fountain, and fell headlong onto the beggar and child. Elif, who was still outside, heard the sound of flesh on stone.

'Get inside!' the girl snatched at her and pulled her in and somebody rammed the shutter down.

The pursuers were on the man who had fallen before he could rise, but no, it was not him they were chasing after all. Crawling on hands and knees, with his face bloody and twisted with fury he was pointing and shouting, 'To the right! To the right!' Some of the crowd wheeled round that way with a renewed roar. Others scattered into the alleyways kicking aside whatever was in their way, as violent and indifferent as a flood tide.

It was very quiet in the shop, until one or two began to speak in whispers.

'Whatever was that? Were they after a thief?'

'It must be thieves. What with the gold market just round the corner.'

'It isn't thieves,' said the elderly man, 'it's war and it's a shame on all of us. That's what it is.' Before anyone could reply another gang of men surged past. These were armed with sticks and broken bottles and lengths of pipe.

Elif watched in horror as the man by the fountain got up. Holding a handful of the newspapers to his head to staunch the blood, he continued to point out the way.

'Who are they?' she whispered to the girl. 'What's happening?'

The girl shrugged and pulled a face. The man who had fallen was coming towards them, swaying and stumbling, his face hidden by the newspaper and the blood.

'I can't move the shutters,' cried Elif, struggling with the weight of them. 'Help me, please.' She knew that he was coming to them.

'Leave the shutters alone,' shouted the elderly man.

'Why? He needs help. He's hurt.' Everyone was looking at her.

'That's one of İbrahim Bey's young men. He won't come to me for help. He's not welcome here.'

'Why?'

No one replied.

The injured man steadied himself against the shop front. Elif turned away, but the elderly man had been right: he was not coming to them for help. He regained his balance, and began to limp away. When the sodden newspaper had fallen from his face Elif recognized him. It was Gülfidan's brother, and Atilla's new friend, Yusuf.

11

Beneath the Surface of the Sea

'I saw your friend today.' Elif put her head round Atilla's bedroom door. She had to shout.

'What friend?' He was sprawled on his bed listening to tapes.

'Gülfidan's brother, Yusuf.'

'So what?' He took off the headphones.

'I saw him in Kapılı Çarşı.'

'What were you doing there?'

'I was looking for you. I wanted to see where you worked and what this İbrahim Bey was like.'

'So?' He smiled jauntily.

'I didn't get that far. I saw the fight.'

'Oh *that*. It wasn't a real fight. We wanted to give them a good beating, but the filthy dogs ran away.' He sat up excitedly. 'Next time . . .'

'What do you mean, "next time"?'

'Next time they do something we don't like, we'll . . . we'll kill them. Honestly, Elif, people like that don't deserve to live!'

'How can you say such things? Anyway, it was horrible, Ati, really horrible. I had to come away and I don't want you involved in things like that. Honestly, you're the last person who should be caught up in such stuff.'

'What do you mean?'

'Have you forgotten what happened in England?'

'No!' He scowled, then glanced furtively at her. 'What *did* happen in England, Elif?'

'So you *have* forgotten! How convenient: you told me that some boys had chased you in the streets after school. They really scared you.'

'Oh *that*. That was nothing, just kid's stuff.'

'But you were terrified! You said that they were out to get you.'

'I wasn't terrified.'

'You were! You sat on the beach that morning and you shook, Ati. You even imagined that some total stranger in a yacht might be coming to "get" you. One of those boys was called Price, you said.'

'Oh shut up.'

'I won't shut up: Price and Hooper, those were their names. I'm right, aren't I?'

'No! Anyway, I made it up.' He tried to put the earphones back on but she snatched them off.

'You made it up?' She didn't believe him.

'Yes. No – I don't know. Just go away, Elif.'

'I shan't, so you've got to listen to me.'

'I haven't!' The words broke from him in a scream that surprised them both. For one second they were children again, watching the door, expecting a grown-up to come in and be cross with them, but nobody seemed to have heard.

'I don't have to listen to you,' he continued. 'I don't have to listen to anyone. Not now. So I *won't*, Elif. I won't.' He wasn't screaming, but the intensity of these whispered words frightened her even more.

'Is that what İbrahim Bey told you?' She hardly knew where the question came from but it lay between them like a scratch across glass.

'Maybe,' he muttered and the nervous smile which flickered over his face told her that her guess was correct.

'Honestly, Elif, İbrahim Bey is an incredible man. He

knows everything.' He was looking into her face, searching for approval. Did he still yearn to feel her arm around his shoulder and the touch of her hand on his forehead as she stroked down his hair?

Years ago, on a hot summer afternoon, she had been standing with the parents by the finishing line at his sport's day. He had been way behind the others in the race: a frantic, awkward child, all jutting elbows and legs as thin as twigs, who had muddled up the instructions and run the wrong route for a moment and so could never have caught up. But he'd run towards her outstretched arms. She had wiped the tears of disappointment from his crimson cheeks and whispered to him that he could have won, almost. He'd sniffed and nodded and his thumping heart had beat hotly against hers. Then she'd smoothed back his damp hair.

'What does İbrahim Bey know?' she asked gently.

'Everything.'

She waited.

'Things about . . . you know . . . about everything. About Turkey, especially plots and things, by foreigners and communists. Americans mostly, İbrahim Bey says. They are trying to make our country weak. Then we'll have to do what they want.'

She listened incredulously. It was the sort of rubbish you heard in the playground.

'You see, Turkey gets pushed around, by Greeks, by Kurds, by communists, by everybody, İbrahim Bey says. You wouldn't understand, Elif, not properly, because you're only a girl, but it's true. We're surrounded by enemies, but men like İbrahim Bey and Yusuf aren't going to allow it. They're going to stand up to all these people, especially the traitors, Elif!'

'What traitors?'

'They're the worst. They're Turks who won't believe what we tell them and won't do the right things. They're filth, Elif, absolute filth.'

'But those people in Kapılı Çarşı, the thieves . . .'

'They weren't thieves. They were traitors or communists or Kurds, probably all three. We couldn't be absolutely sure, but İbrahim Bey recognized them the moment they walked past the shop and luckily Gülfidan Abla's brother, Yusuf, saw which way they'd gone. We'd have caught them, if they hadn't got away. But it's what you'd expect from traitors, isn't it, that they'd sneak away?' His eyes shone with excitement.

'About Price – '

'Who's Price?' He looked puzzled, as if he really had forgotten.

'Did you really make it all up? About Price and Hooper, back in England?'

'No! Are you calling me a liar?'

'Of course not. I just wondered. I need to know the truth.'

'Why? England's all in the past. Refik Abi says that it doesn't matter any more.'

'It matters to me,' she said.

'You? Who cares about you?'

'But . . .'

'It's me they're interested in. That's what İbrahim Bey says. He says that he knew I was the man for the job the moment Refik Bey brought me into his shop.' He stretched himself full length on his bed and put his hands under his head.

'What job, Ati?'

'Wouldn't you like to know!' He tone was suddenly as playful as if they were back in England, and teasing each other about secret Christmas presents.

'What job?' she repeated, but he pretended not to hear.

From outside the door Elif heard suppressed laughter.

'Who's there?' she asked although she had already guessed.

'Me!' Hakan burst in, followed by his brother. 'You've got to play with us. Now!' he cried.

'Now?' protested Elif wearily. 'But it must be past your bedtime.'

'Not you,' Hakan pushed past her. 'We want Atilla Abi.'

A few minutes later the whole house echoed with the sound of their shrieks as Atilla chased them up and down the stairs in a game of cops and robbers. It could only be played properly, he said, in the dark.

Three cold, clear days followed. One morning Hakan ran back in to tell them that there was something stuck on a puddle in the street. Elif went down with him to have a look. It was a thin sheet of ice. Sevim, who never left the house now, insisted that this was the coldest Istanbul winter she'd ever known. She was anxious about the coming baby, though of course, they were warm enough in the house. Refik Bey told them to keep the garden gate locked. Poor people were coming into the city from the shanty towns and stealing anything that burnt. A neighbour, he said, had lost all his garden furniture and half his fence in the night and nobody had heard a thing. Zehra Hanım said that if it kept on like this, the Bosphorus would freeze over and then they'd be able to walk from one shore to the other. The newspapers had reported that birds were dropping from the trees, frozen solid, in the middle of the night. Gülfidan brought news of two drunkards who had crept under an upturned boat to sleep it off, only to be found by fishermen next morning, blue as ink and stiff as boards.

Elif, choosing a moment when she was alone with her

sister, asked awkwardly if she could borrow a little money. There were a few things she needed, and with this un-expectedly cold weather, she'd thought of buying some wool. She wanted to knit a scarf for Atilla and something for the baby too. A shawl, maybe? They could be New Year presents. Sevim blinked rapidly then reached over to take her purse from down the side of the sofa.

'What colour would you like for the baby?'

Her elder sister shrugged disinterestedly. She had spent most of the week lying on the sofa. Her ankles had swollen up and she had no energy at all. Gülfidan did everything in the house.

'I could get something that wasn't pink. It might not be a girl,' Elif suggested. They both looked at the huge bump. Elif still felt uncomfortable when she thought about it. How could her sister lie there so indifferently waiting for this amazing thing to happen to her? They never spoke about it and when, occasionally, Elif saw the baby kick and shift, Sevim plucked at the folds of her long dress so that nothing more showed.

'How about green?' Elif continued, 'Or even navy blue. I saw lots of babies in England in navy blue, with stripes. They looked so sweet.' Sevim wasn't listening. She opened the purse and held out some money without counting it.

'If it isn't enough, ask Refik Bey tomorrow,' Sevim murmured. 'He'll buy whatever you want. And better quality than you can get locally. Unless . . .' she hesitated. The silk scarf had slipped and she fiddled with the knot. 'Unless . . . you want to go and look. Locally.' For once Sevim met her gaze.

'Would that be all right, Sevim?' For a moment Elif wondered if her sister knew about Yaşar and the wool shop next door.

'Why not?' The reply was scarcely audible and Sevim almost smiled as she handed over the notes. Outside, although it was winter, the midday sun was dazzling. Sevim blinked again and reached out to pull a curtain across. As she did so her scarf slipped off.

'Sevim! Whatever's the matter . . . with your hair?' There were bare patches all over her sister's head, where the skin shone through palely, and in one place there was a streak of dried blood.

'Nothing's the matter. It's . . . the baby.' Sevim hurriedly retied the scarf and smoothed it down. She settled herself further into the corner where the shade was deepest and she shut her eyes, as though suddenly overwhelmed by sleep.

'Sevim?'

'Mm?' Her sister's closed face was as impassive as if she really had fallen asleep; only her tightly clenched hands betrayed her.

'Sevim? What happened?'

Her sister wouldn't reply and with growing unease Elif put the money in her pocket and left the house.

This time she didn't bother about walking by the sea. She went as swiftly as she could along the coast road and in less time than expected was approaching the square. The sun still shone sharply on the trunks of the plane trees and on the windows of the three shops. Now that she was here she didn't know what to do next. Each time she thought she had reached some understanding, everything changed again and she was as confused as before. She walked over to the wool shop and tried to concentrate on the selection. The turquoise was beautiful and that was all she needed to think about. She could begin work that evening. She imagined the new baby wrapped up snugly in a turquoise shawl that would be the colour of the sea off Taşlı Ada, where there were no black rocks underneath . . .

'Elif! Welcome back!'

She had pushed open the door of the spice shop without even noticing. He came from behind the counter to greet her.

'I didn't mean to come.' She couldn't return his smile or shake his hand. The sudden warmth of the shop made her eyes water.

'What's the matter?'

'It's . . . it's my sister.' It wasn't what she had intended to say. She had planned, if anything, to talk about Atilla.

'Your sister? Has she had the baby? Is she all right?'

'No, no. It's not that. It's . . .'

He waited, returning to what he had been doing and weighing out neat 250 gram amounts of something that looked like black pepper.

'Yaşar, what exactly happened on that trip to Taşlı Ada?'

'I told you.'

'You haven't told me everything, have you?'

'No.' He was gaining time, folding down the tops of the packets and sealing them with sellotape.

'Tell me. Please.'

He laid aside the work.

'Sevim said, well, I *thought* she said, "Let me go." '

'But . . . she couldn't have . . .'

'I'd got hold of her dress first. I can still remember the feel of it, so cold and heavy on that hot day. Then I grabbed her hand, and that's when she said it. She said, "Let me go." '

'You could have made a mistake.'

'Yes. And I've always wondered if I did, but there was no one to ask. Ahmet Efendi said that he knew the marriage wasn't happy but he was only an employee and I was only a boy. It was nothing to do with us. Hatice Teyze laughed and said, what did people expect, when a schoolgirl was married to a man more than twice her age? So I kept quiet, but that was when I really began to dislike Refik Bey, though it was only personal then. He was unpleasant to me, the lad who helped in the garden, and now I suspected that his young wife was so unhappy that she might have tried to drown herself. But so what? She wasn't *my* sister. I went back to Germany and I forgot all about it. Why should I be haunted by one unhappy girl, one bully of a husband and one spoiled summer afternoon? I didn't think about it again until I saw you last summer.'

'Me?'

He nodded but didn't look at her. He had begun to write out labels and was sticking them on rapidly.

'I didn't want the same thing to happen to you. And by then of course, I knew about Refik Bey.'

'Knew what?'

'Do you remember I told you about my elder brother, Ferhat, the journalist? We're very close, he and I. He's always looked out for me especially when we were kids in Germany. When we came back from there and began to work in the family business, Ferhat carried on writing. He'd started a bit in Germany, writing about Turkish workers there and the problems of migrant labour and so on. Well, when he travelled around Turkey on business, buying the produce that we sell, he continued writing. At first it was mainly humorous stories and anecdotes about country life, but it was very popular. Lots of people who've moved into cities looking for work, and an education for their children and all that, still have memories of life back in their villages. Families who've been in towns for several generations still have someone, somewhere who is working on the land.

They liked what Ferhat wrote. He built up a huge readership but when he began writing about poverty and inequality and land ownership, he began to make enemies. When he wrote a story about the man who collects the orchid roots for salep, nobody minded, but when he wrote about poverty in the South or about the Kurds or the Armenians, then he was in big trouble. Powerful men like your brother-in-law and İbrahim Bey don't want to see any discussion of controversial things in newspapers. They think they're right and they don't want to be questioned, especially not by some popular journalist like Ferhat who keeps on asking awkward questions.'

'Why do you call Refik Bey "powerful"?'

'Because he is! His money originally came from cotton in the South. He has clothing factories and so on. Now he's into banking and finance as well and he gives huge amounts to the right-wing politicians he agrees with. İbrahim Bey works out of the gold market in Kapılı Çarşı. He also runs a network of foreign exchange booths down there, where tourists change their foreign money into Turkish lira. It's a huge business.'

'And?'

'And . . . he manages the local branch of a right-wing political party. Fascists they are. You know the sort of thing, "Turkey for Turks". There were fascist parties in Germany and I bet it's the same in England, but that doesn't make it any better. All the young men İbrahim Bey employs are involved in the party. Ferhat has written articles about it, how they organize themselves by looking out for young lads . . .' He stopped himself suddenly and began stacking one of the shelves.

'Lads like Atilla. That's what you were going to say, wasn't it?'

'Yes. I'm so sorry. In the beginning, when Ahmet Efendi told me that you weren't going back to England, I thought it was *you* they wanted.'

'Me? Why me? I'd be hopeless at that sort of business. Anyway, I didn't see many girls working in Kapılı Çarşı!'

'I didn't mean *that* sort of business.'

Then she understood.

'You've met Yusuf?' Yaşar continued. 'Refik Bey's right-hand man? He's not married: a nice looking young fellow, plenty of money, good prospects, very moral, never drinks – he could do with a wife . . .'

'But he's disgusting!'

'Maybe not him, especially, but someone like that. Anyway that's what I thought, to begin with.'

'To begin with?'

'I changed my mind when I saw you that day in the market, when you were going to buy coach tickets. I realized that if they were seriously planning to arrange a marriage they'd never have left you on your own like that. After all, in their eyes, girls can't be trusted on their own.'

'So Atilla was right!'

Now Yaşar looked puzzled.

'It's something he said the other day. He said that nobody was interested in me, and he was right. They wanted *him* all along, but they used me, didn't they? They saw how close we were. They knew that he needed me, that if I stayed, he'd stay too. They never wanted me at all. I was just like . . . bait. But why, Yaşar? Why him?'

'Well, he's got good English and he's young and easily influenced. He's family, so they can control him better, and he's weak, isn't he? Hopelessly weak. He'll do anything.'

Terror swept over her and she could not hold it back. In

the end Yaşar agreed to close the shop and go with her to look for her brother.

12

The Colour of Gold

A taxi dropped them at a different entrance to Kapılı Çarşı and within minutes they were in the gold market. The glitter and the brightness of it dazzled her. It was like the sun spun out as fine as thread and twisted and worked but then wound round and round. Refik Bey must have bought the bangle here.

It was busy, too. People gave gifts of gold at New Year. Crowds milled to and fro. A beggar, propped on a wooden cart, called to her. He had no arms and no legs and was tied there with a length of rope to stop him slipping. As Elif watched a small child, sent by its mother, trotted over and put money in the beggar's box.

'Look.' Yaşar touched her arm.

Beyond the beggar, a young man stood in the door of a shop. Even before Elif had seen his bruised face she knew that it was Yusuf. She would have run forward if Yaşar hadn't pulled her back.

They watched from across the alley until the shop was almost empty of customers, then Elif crossed over to it. Yaşar returned to wait at a café they had passed near the entrance. It would be a good place to wait. He knew it well as he often met friends there. Once Elif had persuaded Atilla to leave work for half an hour she was to bring him to the café. It wasn't much of a plan but it was the best she could think of.

Now that she was about to enter the shop, she felt herself

to be the one who was weak. When she had insisted on coming she had imagined herself marching in and reclaiming Atilla like lost property: she would put a protective arm around his shoulders and lead him away. He might protest at first, and so might İbrahim Bey, a crowd might gather to watch their exit, but Atilla would come with her. He always did. And, secretly, he would be relieved. He would finally recognize that she was right and that their original, childish dislike of Refik Bey had been well founded. He was not a man to trust.

She imagined them running back to the café together. Atilla would be confessing, in breathless gasps, that he hadn't really liked working in the shop, but that he hadn't known how to get out of it. She, as always, had forced open the iron teeth and released him just in time. He would squeeze her hand and they would run even faster, just in case they were being chased. But it would be all right.

When she glanced behind her, Yaşar had disappeared into the crowds. A balloon seller was coming towards her. The bobbing, pulling mass was too big for the confined alley-way. Some people protested, others stopped to buy. A tangle of small children followed after, willing one balloon, at least, to break free. For a moment, the relentless flickering gold in the shop window was patterned over with the colours of everyday life.

She could see Atilla now. He reached between the rows of gold bangles, biting his lip with concentration, trying not to disturb anything. Yusuf had returned to the till. An older man sat at the back of the shop. He must be Ibrahim Bey. Yet whatever could she say?

Then Atilla saw her. Startled, he withdrew his arm too quickly, and knocked the corner of a glass shelf. She thought that everything would crash down. The bangles swayed and swung against each other and at this rasp of sound the other men looked up too. Nothing fell. Atilla scowled, but Yusuf smiled and came out to greet her.

'Why, Elif Hanım! What a surprise – a pleasant surprise, and an honour.' It could have been Gülfidan speaking. 'Atilla, why didn't you tell us your sister was coming?' Yusuf's smile was uneven because the recent scar pulled the skin too tightly.

'I forgot,' Atilla muttered.

'It wasn't ... definite,' added Elif and then wondered why she had supported his lie. 'I was passing and wondered if Ati could have five minutes off. For tea with me.' It was more difficult than she had imagined.

'But of course,' Yusuf fingered the ridges in the scar, 'only you must be *our* guest. Mustn't she, İbrahim Bey?'

'Indeed she must.' The older man's cold eyes darted amongst their faces like the breathless tongue of a snake.

'I can't come in,' she took a deeper breath. 'Ati and I have to talk about something. In private.'

'Is that so?' There was undisguised suspicion in Ibrahim Bey's voice, as if she had pointed to a flaw in his gold.

'Yes, it is.' She spoke as firmly as she could.

'I can't come.' Atilla turned away sulkily.

'Why not?' She wasn't going to give him up. 'He can come, can't he?' They all avoided her glance until Yusuf, smiling still, stepped between them.

'Of course he can come. Atilla, get your jacket. We can all go. This is an opportunity for me. I can learn more about England. Isn't that so? We can go to a café, if you don't want to remain here ...'

She couldn't prevent it. At each further step she wondered why she didn't pretend to faint, or trip, or do anything, rather than keep on walking towards the café.

Yusuf was nodding to people on his right and left. They passed the balloon seller, then skirted a group around a lad selling clockwork beetles. She didn't even hang back and watch as the toys scuttled briefly before tumbling into cracks with their black plastic legs whirring ineffectually in the air. They walked on, side by side, with Elif in the middle, as though they were three friends.

Yaşar wasn't alone. He was sitting outside with the collar of his coat turned up, at one of the tables which caught a little winter sun. As Elif approached a waiter went by with coffees swinging on a round brass tray. He stopped by Yaşar, taking the saucers from the top of the cups and setting one before Yaşar and the other before Ferhat, who still stood and pointed encouragingly to the tables inside, in the warm. She saw the trails of steam, saw Yaşar grin and point to the seat. He was shaking his head and laughing but refusing to go in to the warm, because of her. Ferhat was laughing too as he sat down.

'Do you see who *that* is?' Yusuf had stopped suddenly.

'Who? Who?' Atilla pushed Elif aside and stood close to Yusuf. Elif could hear their panting breath. Yusuf's red tongue licked round his lips and he whispered hoarsely into Atilla's ear:

'That's Ferhat Güney, the journalist!'

Atilla's fists clenched.

'Look at him, sitting there as though he owned the place! He'll be collecting more lies to write about us. Look at him, sniffing around like the dog he is, and on our patch!'

Atilla started forward. Yusuf clung on for a moment before Atilla jerked free. From nowhere another youth joined them. Then two more. Out there, where it was bright after the dimness of the alley-ways, Ferhat tilted his chair back. He had shut his eyes and raised his face to the sun's warmth. He did not see them coming towards him. Yaşar had lifted the cup to his lips and had the soft, sweet froth of the coffee in his mouth when he looked up. At first there were only those five men. They were taunting the brothers, hurling abuse at them and howling their hate. Chairs and tables were overturned as people fled into doorways and crouched down behind walls. A cook in an apron rushed from the café and stood between them, flapping a kitchen cloth and begging them to keep calm. More men arrived and he was knocked down in the sudden, violent rush. Elif saw Yaşar fall too.

'Stop it!' she screamed. 'Stop it!' But no one did. No one even heard her.

For a moment Ferhat seemed to be holding them off. He stood over Yaşar, swinging a chair round in front of him but his attackers were beyond fear. They had got behind him and there were too many of them and they fell on him with eager, savage cries. When they drew back he did not get up.

Later, when the police finally arrived, there was only a stain of blood on the flagstones. Everyone else, Yusuf and Atilla among them, had vanished. Elif, watching from behind a pillar, saw the cook come out again. His apron was soiled and his shirt torn. Stiffly he righted the chairs and tables and picked up bits of broken glass with a trembling hand. Then he threw down a bucket of water and swept at the mark, until it had gone, but Elif could see others where Yaşar and the waiter had stumbled to a taxi with Ferhat sprawled between them.

Elif knew that she should leave too. Yaşar would be at the hospital. He could not come back for her. Not now. She should just walk away, but when she tried, she couldn't begin to take a step. A couple of passers-by asked if she was all right. It was shock, they said. She should sit down, have a glass of water. Was she really all right? She nodded. Yes, she was fine and no, she hadn't actually seen what happened, but it was still a shock. She agreed to go home, but didn't move. She steadied herself against the pillar and when someone else stopped she lied and replied that she was only waiting for her parents. That was all.

In the gold market the police were going from shop to shop. They would reach her soon. Someone would point her out: 'That's the girl,' they would shout, 'that's the young girl who led those men straight to Ferhat Güney! I remember her because she doesn't look like a Turk! There's no mistake, that's the girl who betrayed him!'

When they reached her, however, they walked past and would not have questioned her at all if she hadn't spoken out.

'That man,' she began, 'the one they murdered – '

'Murdered?' one of them paused. 'No one's been murdered. Not yet. We're investigating a fight, not a murder. So don't upset yourself.'

'I thought . . . a man was . . . hurt.'

'That's right. Stabbed. But I don't think he'll die. I don't suppose you saw who did it?'

'Not exactly.'

'Well, there you are then. You shouldn't worry.' He looked at her kindly. 'And you shouldn't hang about here, there's always trouble.' He shook his head glumly and hurried after his colleagues into the next shop. Elif rested her cheek wearily against the rough carved stone.

'Well done, young lady!' İbrahim Bey sidled round the other side of the pillar. 'That was *so* wise: it's best not to get involved.'

'Where's my brother?' The sight of him disgusted her.

'He's safe. For now.'

'Safe?'

'That's what I said. He's safe, for the moment. And since you didn't see anything, it seems that you are safe, too.'

She heard the menace in his voice and tried to avoid his eyes. He bent closer still and whispered hotly into her face:

'And if you did see anything, anything at all, then I advise you, young lady, to forget it. For your brother's sake, if not for your own.'

'For my brother's sake?'

'That's right,' he smiled, 'if you love your little brother you'll forget all about this.'

Fear closed around her and when he told her that he had arranged for her to be taken home she nodded and climbed into the car as obediently as any frightened child.

Atilla was not in the house. She hurried from room to room calling his name. Zehra Hanım and Sevim, who were watching the television news, looked up irritably. What was all the fuss about? It was barely evening and Atilla never came home at this time.

'And where's the wool?' asked Zehra Hanım.

'What wool?' Elif had forgotten. On the screen a news-caster announced increased tourism in Istanbul.

'Sevim said you were getting wool for a shawl. I must say, I've never known anyone take so long to choose a ball of wool! People might think you didn't want to be in the house with us.'

Elif ignored the old lady's tone. She was struggling back through the impossible hours to the moment when she was last in this room and had talked about the colours of wool. She would never be that person again.

'Well, did you get it?' Sevim pointed to some magazines. 'I found some patterns. Look.'

Did Sevim really have no knowledge of what had happened?

'Make *me* something,' urged Hakan, 'knit me something *first*.' He snatched at a magazine and danced off holding it out of reach of Volkan who ran behind him and cried. Sevim sighed and protested, but the little boys took no notice.

The television changed from news to a cartoon. The children settled down. Outside it was almost dark. Gülfidan was late coming over to begin the evening meal.

'I went to Kapılı Çarşı this afternoon,' Elif said loudly, 'and I saw something.'

No one looked away from the cartoon. Maybe they genuinely didn't know. When she told them what had happened, they would be shocked and they would understand her fears about Atilla.

'I saw – ' she began again, but her voice failed as Refik Bey unexpectedly entered the room.

'You saw?' he repeated. He was still dressed in his outdoor clothes. He hadn't even changed his shoes. The key with which he'd silently let himself in still lay in his hand.

'Come along, Elif. Do tell us what you saw in Kapılı Çarşı – if you think it right to bring such stories into the heart of a family.'

'But I *saw* it, Refik Abi! I saw them attack . . . that poor man!'

'What man?' asked Zehra Hanım.

'Oh just some journalist,' Refik Bey's voice was dismissive, but his eyes never left Elif's face. 'It was that Ferhat Güney,' I think.'

'Oh *him*.' The old woman turned back to the cartoon. 'About time someone did something to that man. Whenever I read his articles he upsets me. People shouldn't be allowed to write stuff like that! Do you know, Elif, he wrote things about Refik Bey, even after he'd been warned not to! Serves him right, the interfering journalist! I should forget about it, Elif, if I were you. Now, where's Gülfidan? She knows how delicate my digestion is. I shall be up all night if my supper's late. Gülfidan!' Her shout rang through the house.

'Sevim?' begged Elif, but her sister would not look up. She was busy turning the new bangle round and round on her white wrist.

The evening hours dragged by. Atilla's place remained empty but no one commented. Nor did they notice that Elif hardly ate anything at all. It was as though she wasn't there, as though some other girl crumbled the bread and watched the hands of the clock tick slowly on. At ten she pleaded tiredness and went upstairs.

She waited in darkness in Atilla's room and when he finally came in, long past midnight, she had decided what she must do. She had dozed off but jerked awake continually with the horror of it. In the guest house window the light still glowed. That, of course, was where he was. He had been there all evening and everybody had known except her. They knew, just as they knew what Refik Bey and his friends were involved in: they knew and they didn't care.

Finally she had heard something. Gülfidan's tall figure was outlined as she stood aside for a group of men who hurried silently down the steps to a waiting car. Atilla, creeping out afterwards, came up to the house alone. She heard his footsteps on the stairs.

'Elif!' He had entered his own room like a thief, feeling his way, without putting on the light until safely inside. He was pale with dark circles under his eyes. His mouth and nose were swollen. He had been crying. Now the light revealed him to be dressed from head to foot in brand new clothes. He smiled an uncertain, embarrassed smile as though she had caught him trying on somebody else's outfit.

'Did you stab him?' she asked.

'Do what?' He was searching her face, needing her to smile back. 'Do *what*?' His neck was twisting uncomfortably as though a pin were left inside the new collar.

'Did you, Ati?' For the first time in her life she did not want to run over to him and put her arms around him.

'Did you, Ati?'

'Not really!' He swallowed. 'Not as much as the others. It was just *fun*, just – fun.'

She longed for him to explain so that she could go on loving him, just a little bit, but as she watched, something clouded his face. He swore angrily.

'I knew it,' he scowled, 'they've given me a blister already!' He untied the laces of the new shoes. 'I told Yusuf that they were too tight but he wouldn't listen. He said it didn't matter. Do you know, Elif, I don't think they care what happens to me. Not really.' He began to peel off his sock. When he looked up Elif had left the room. He called her name, but with frantic, trembling hands she drew the bolt across her door.

Dawn was breaking when she left the house. A yellow winter sun hung over the city and for a short while a golden glow lay on the smoothed waters of the Bosphorus. Around her the call to prayer filtered through the chill air and mingled with the first thin smoke of early morning fires.

She made her way towards the coast road. Although it was deserted she was no longer so afraid. Some link in the chain of fear that had held her was broken.

There was no one about. Near the park an old dog

140

dragged on something hanging from the rubbish in an oil drum. It tugged again, going down on its haunches, its swollen teats flapping against the ground. From close by she heard the mew of pups. Beyond, in the park, the roundabout and swings were almost obscured by mist. She imagined her hand gripping the wet, black metal and the bite of the iron handles on a bitter morning like this. Then she remembered that other sunny day in the South when her brother had been pushing Noyan on the swing. What had Atilla accused her of? Spoiling his 'fun', that was it.

Fun?

And she, fool that she was, had wondered if he was right!

Somewhere, something moved. She heard a sound and looked back towards the house. Had the gate swung shut in this windless dawn where only the mist moved as it drifted over the sea?

Then the oil drum overturned. It crashed down, striking the row of railings before rolling into the road where it scattered out ash and broken glass and rusting cans. The dog leapt aside, then, when all was quiet again, it moved back in and began to scratch out last night's bones. Unseen, the little pups called again. That was all it had been; Atilla hadn't come after her. She brushed back her hair and pushed her cold hands into her pockets and began to walk briskly away without looking back.

Atilla was not the one who was out at dawn. He had stayed there and stretched out more comfortably on his bed; in the morning he would put on the new clothes and pause at the front door while Gülfidan bent to flick the dust from his newly polished shoes. Then he would follow Refik Bey out to the car.

The mist had dampened her cheeks so she wiped her

sleeve over her face. Then she shook out her hair and raked her fingers through the curls, and began to walk along the road beside the sea. When she got to the square the first rays of sun would be shining on the plane trees, and that was where she could wait, at one of the green tables outside, until the shops opened up and she could go in to the warm. She quickened her pace and smiled at a young boy who was out searching for driftwood along the shore and she suddenly realized that nothing could ever force her to walk back along that road again.

Glossary of Turkish Words

abla	elder sister; used after woman's name to indicate respect
Altın Ada	Gold Island
aslan	lion
Bey	gentleman; used after name to indicate Mr, e.g. Refik Bey
dolmuş	taxi which only operates when full of passengers
Dur!	Stop!
Efendi	gentleman; used after name, indicates servant, lower class, e.g. Ahmet Efendi
gofre	wafer biscuit
Hanım	lady, woman; used after name to indicate Mrs, Miss, e.g. Filiz Hanım
helva	sweet made from sesame and sugar
İngiliz	English
İnşallah	God willing; used for 'I hope so'
Kapılı Çarşı	covered bazaar
kardeşler	brothers, sisters
köfte	meat ball
küçük	little
küçük İngiliz	little English girl
lokum	Turkish delight
maşallah	used to express wonder: God Bless; to avert evil eye
nâne	mint
nâne şekeri	peppermint drop
pide	slightly leavened flat bread
şalvar	baggy trousers
şeker	sugar

şeriat	Islamic canonical law
simit	ring-shaped bread roll
tarhana	soup made from dried curds, flour and seasoning
taşlı	stony
Taşlı Ada	Stony Island
testi	earthenware pitcher
teyze	maternal aunt; used after woman's name to indicate close relationship, e.g. Hatice Teyze.
ve	and
Yakala!	Arrest him!

PROPER NAMES

Elif	
Atilla	Elif's younger brother
Sevim	Elif's elder sister
Filiz Hanım	Elif's mother
Refik Bey	Sevim's husband
Zehra Hanım	Refik's mother
Hakan	Sevim's elder son
Volkan	Sevim's younger son
Ahmet Efendi	caretaker
Hatice Teyze	Ahmet Efendi's wife
Noyan	their little grandson
Ferhat Güney	journalist, Ahmet Efendi's grandson
Yaşar Güney	Ferhat's younger brother
Gülfidan Akbulut	domestic servant
Ömer Akbulut	her husband
Yusuf	Gülfidan's brother
İbrahim Bey	businessman in Kapılı Çarşı

Note regarding spelling and pronunciation of Turkish words:

Ç, ç is pronounced 'ch', as in *ch*air
C, c is pronounced 'j', as in John
Ş, ş is pronounced 'sh', as in *sh*oe

In Turkish, the *i* and the *ı* are separate letters:

İ, i is pronounced 'i', as in 't*i*n
I, ı is pronounced 'uh', as in the last syllable of construct*i*on

Also by Gaye Hiçyılmaz

Against the Storm
Shortlisted for the Whitbread Award and
Guardian Young Fiction Award

Mehmet's family moves from a blossom-filled village to a derelict
shanty town in Ankara, and Mehmet has to learn a new way of
surviving life on the streets – fast. As he grows older he begins to
recognize the trap that poverty has sprung around him. With
help and friendship from Hayri, starving and half mad, as well
as Muhlis, an enterprising orphan, he nurtures plans to escape to
a better life.

The Frozen Waterfall
Winner of the Writers' Guild Award Best Children's Book
Shortlisted for the Smarties Award and
Guardian Young Fiction Award

Selda feels completely uprooted when she moves with her mother
and sisters from Turkey to live with her father in Switzerland. At
school, she can neither understand the language nor the lifestyle
of the people around her. But Selda is a fighter. Her independence
and strength of spirit gain her an unlikely set of friends, and as
she is increasingly drawn into their lives, she finds herself forced
to make a decision between her old life and a new beginning.

Watching the Watcher

Henry feels as comfortable in his 'nice' family as a splinter stuck
under a fingernail and he welcomes the chance to stay with his
uncle, the naturalist Arthur Constable. But behind the high wire
fences of his uncle's nature reserve lies a terrible hidden secret
and only crimson-haired Stella seems to know the truth. As the
story unfolds, Henry's feelings for Stella swing in bewildering
turns from love to hate.